ROCHDALE
METROPOLITAN BOROUGH
COUNCIL

Please return/renew this item
by the last date shown.
Books may also be renewed by

phone: 03003038876 or web

www.rochdale.gov.uk/libraries

A D'ANGELO
LIKE NO OTHER

A D'ANGELO LIKE NO OTHER

BY

CAROLE MORTIMER

MILLS & BOON®

First published in Great Britain 2014
by Mills & Boon, an imprint of Harlequin (UK) Limited,
Large Print edition 2014
Eton House, 18-24 Paradise Road,
Richmond, Surrey, TW9 1SR

© 2014 Carole Mortimer

ISBN: 978-0-263-24081-8

Printed and bound in Great Britain
by CPI Antony Rowe, Chippenham, Wiltshire

Our Son, Matthew, A Man to be Proud of.

PROLOGUE

St Gregory's Church, New York.

'WEREN'T THE THREE of us sitting together in a church very like this one just a few weeks ago?' Michael spoke mockingly to his youngest brother Gabriel as they sat in the front pew of the church crowded with wedding guests, their restless brother Rafe seated on his other side.

'I believe we were, yes,' Gabriel confirmed dryly. 'Except on that occasion you and Rafe were my best men, and now we're Rafe's.'

'How many weeks ago was that, exactly?' Michael arched derisive brows.

'Five wonderful, glorious weeks.' Gabriel smiled at the thought of his own recent marriage to his beloved Bryn.

'Hmm.' Michael nodded. 'Did I ever tell you of the conversation I had with Rafe that day, in which he assured me, most emphatically I believe, that he didn't believe in this "one love of a lifetime" thing, and certainly had no intention of getting married in the immediate, or even distant, future?'

Gabriel glanced at their brother Rafe, holding back a smile as he saw the tension in Rafe's white face as he waited for his bride to arrive at the church. 'No, I don't believe you did…'

'Oh, yes.' Michael settled more comfortably on the pew. 'It was as we were standing outside the church together, when you and Bryn were posing for photographs. I seem to remember that Rafe had just received a call from one of his women, and—'

'And this is hardly the time, or the place, for you to so much as mention any of that!' A tense Rafe turned on them both fiercely, his brief relationship with the Parisian, Monique, having ended several months before he had even met his future bride.

The three D'Angelo brothers owned and ran the three prestigious Archangel galleries and auction houses, in New York, London and Paris. Until recently they had run those galleries on a casual two-to-three-month-rotation basis, depending on what exhibitions or auctions were taking place in each gallery, but Gabriel's marriage to Bryn now meant that he was based mainly in London, Rafe would be spending most of his time in New York once he and Nina were married, leaving Michael in charge at the Paris gallery.

'Nina is now five minutes late,' Rafe muttered after another glance at his wristwatch, the tenth such glance in almost as few seconds.

'It's the bride's prerogative to keep the man waiting,' Gabriel dismissed unconcernedly. 'A case of "how the mighty have fallen", don't you think?' he calmly continued his conversation with Michael.

'Oh, most definitely.' Michael nodded. 'From what I've observed, he's been totally off his head since the day he met Nina.' He grinned unabashedly in the face of Rafe's scowl.

'Love does that to you.' Gabriel nodded wisely. 'It will be your turn next, Michael.'

His humour instantly faded. 'I don't believe so,' he assured with grim certainty.

'Famous last words…?'

'Fact,' Michael corrected tersely. 'I can't imagine ever willingly allowing any woman to get me into that state.' He gave a pointed glance in Rafe's visibly agitated direction.

'When you two have quite finished!' Rafe's hands had clenched into fists, his expression one of pained tension as he turned to glare at his two brothers. 'Nina is late, damn it!'

'We heard you the first time…' Michael arched one dark brow. 'Do you think she might have changed her mind about marrying you?'

Rafe's already pale face seemed to take on a greyish tinge as he groaned. 'Oh, God…!'

'Stop teasing him, Michael,' Gabriel chided affectionately, his five-week marriage to Bryn having completely mellowed him. 'Personally, I'm longing to see the beautiful matron of honour!' He smiled at the thought of his wife.

Michael shrugged broad shoulders. 'Calm down, Rafe. Nina will be here,' he assured his brother dryly. 'For some strange reason the woman is in love with you!'

'Ha ha, very funny.' Rafe scowled.

'The limo is probably having trouble getting through the New York traffic, that's all.' Michael grimaced.

'Lord, I hope so.' Rafe's face had taken on a

slightly green tinge now. 'I knew I should have gone ahead with my original plan and just persuaded Nina to elope!'

'Not if you had wanted to continue living, Raphael Charles D'Angelo!' his mother warned from the pew directly behind them, the whole of the D'Angelo family having once again gathered together to see another one of the three brothers married.

Which left Michael, the eldest brother at thirty-five, as the only remaining bachelor...

A state he intended to continue!

Oh, Michael was pleased for both of his younger brothers, had absolutely no doubt that Rafe and Gabriel loved the two women they had chosen as their wives, and that those two women loved them in return, that the two couples would have long and happy lives together. It just wasn't a state, the love or the marriage, that Michael wanted for himself.

Ever.

He had been in love precisely once in his life, fourteen years ago, disastrously as it turned out, and it wasn't an experience he had ever felt the slightest inclination to repeat. All that angsting and heartache had just made him miserable, the betrayal even more so, and he certainly hadn't enjoyed the unpleasant feeling of having lost control of his emotions.

A feeling that he would find even more unacceptable after all these years of doing exactly as he pleased, when he pleased, with whomever and whatever woman he pleased.

No, as far as Michael was concerned, Rafe and Gabriel could provide the next generation of D'Angelos, because he had no intention of having his well-ordered life complicated by either a wife or children.

'Oh, thank God…' Rafe breathed his relief as the organist began to play the Wedding March announcing Nina's arrival at the church, the three men standing up to turn and look at the bride as she walked down the aisle at her father's side. Nina was a vision in white satin and lace, her smile radiantly beautiful, love shining in her eyes as she walked towards her bridegroom.

Michael felt a slight pang in his chest as he realised that his decision not to marry meant that no woman would ever gaze at him with such open adoration.

A pang he quickly quashed and buried, in the knowledge that *he* had no intention of ever falling victim to loving any woman in the way his brothers now loved their wives...

CHAPTER ONE

Archangel gallery, Paris. Two days later

'WHAT THE—?' MICHAEL looked up to scowl his displeasure as he heard what sounded like a baby crying in the office opposite his own. He stood up quickly behind his desk as several voices now clamoured to be heard above the noise.

The sound of raised voices, so close to the inner sanctum of Michael's private third-floor office, was unusual enough, but a baby crying…? In one of the private areas of the prestigious Paris Archangel gallery and auction house? It was unheard of! And Michael had little patience for it having occurred now.

He continued to scowl as he strode forcefully across his office to wrench open the door into the hallway, only to come to an abrupt halt, his verbal protest dying in his throat at the pandemonium that met his narrowed gaze.

His secretary, Marie, was fiercely gabbling away in French, as was his assistant manager, Pierre Dupont. Both of them, as was usual with the French, communicating as much with their hands as with their mouths.

And standing between them, holding a young baby in her arms, was a young girl—woman?—with ebony shoulder-length hair, dressed in the *de rigueur* tight denims and fitted T-shirt of her generation. Her top was a bright purple, the expression on her flustered face flushed as she ignored both Marie and Pierre and instead attempted to soothe and cajole the crying baby into silence.

An attempt that failed miserably as the baby's cries seemed to grow even louder.

'Will you two please lower your voices?' The young woman turned impatiently on Marie and Pierre, her voice throatily husky. 'You're scaring her. Now look what you've done…!' she fumed as a second baby began to cry.

Michael looked around dazedly for the source of that second cry, his eyes widening as he noticed the pushchair parked just inside Marie's office. A double pushchair, in which a second baby was now screaming at the top of its considerable lungs.

What the—?

Pandemonium? This situation, whatever that might be, was like some sort of hellish nightmare, the sort every man wished—prayed!—to wake up from. And sooner rather than later!

'Thank you,' the disgruntled young woman muttered accusingly as Marie and Pierre both fell silent as she hurried over to the pushchair before going down on her haunches to coo and attempt to gently soothe the second baby.

Michael had seen and heard enough. 'Will someone, for the love of God, tell me what the hell is going on here?' His voice cut harshly through the cacophony of noise.

Silence.

Absolute blissful silence, Eva realised with a sigh of appreciation for her aching head, as not only the two employees of the Paris Archangel remained silent, but even the babies' cries both quietened down to a soft whimper.

Eva remained down on her haunches as she turned to look through sooty black lashes at the source of that harshly controlling voice, her eyes widening as she took in the appearance of the man standing across the hallway.

He was possibly aged in his mid to late thirties, his short black hair was neatly trimmed about his ears and nape, and framed an olive-skinned and handsomely etched face that any of the male models Eva had photographed at the beginning of her career would surely die for. Dark brows arched above eyes of obsidian black, his nose a long straight slash between high cheekbones, with sculptured, slightly sensual lips above a firm and determined chin.

His wide shoulders, muscled chest, tapered waist, and lean hips above long legs also en-sured that *he* wore the expensively tailored dark suit, white silk shirt and grey tie, rather than the clothes wearing him.

And leaving Eva in no doubt, along with the deference on the faces of the two silent gallery employees, and the fact that he had come from the office across the hallway, that this man had to be D'Angelo. The very man she had come here to see!

It was a realisation that ensured there was absolutely no deference in Eva's own expression as she straightened before crossing the room to thrust Sophie at him. 'Take her so I can get Sam,' she instructed impatiently as he made no effort to lift the baby from her arms but instead looked at her incredulously, down the long length of his aristocratic nose, with those black-on-black eyes.

Michael found himself having to look a long way down. Goodness, this woman was small, only an inch or two over five feet tall compared to his own six feet three inches. She had a coltish slenderness that was saved from appearing boyish by full and thrusting breasts tipped by delicate nipples, breasts that were completely bare beneath the purple T-shirt, if Michael wasn't mistaken. And he was pretty sure that he wasn't.

Those full breasts, along with the confident glint in those violet-coloured eyes surrounded by thick sooty lashes, were enough to tell Michael that she was indeed a woman rather than a girl, and possibly aged in her early to mid-twenties.

She was also, he acknowledged grudgingly, extremely beautiful, her face dominated by those incredible violet-coloured eyes, a short pert nose, and full and sensuous lips, while her skin was as pale and delicate as the finest porcelain. Dark shadows beneath the violet eyes gave her an appearance of fragility.

A fragility that was somewhat nullified by the stubborn set of the woman's full lips above an equally determined and thrusting chin.

Michael dragged his gaze away from that arrestingly beautiful face to instead stare down in horror at the pink-dress-clad baby this young woman held out in front of him; horror, because he had absolutely no experience with holding young babies. How could he have, when he had never been this close to a small baby since being one himself?

He recoiled back from the now-drooling infant. 'I don't think—'

'I've found that it's best not to think too much around Sophie and Sam, especially now they're teething,' he was assured dryly. 'You might want to put this on your shoulder to protect your jacket.'

The woman handed him a square of white linen as she dumped the baby unceremoniously into his arms before turning to stride back across the office, giving Michael a perfect view of her curvaceous denim-covered bottom as she bent down to unclip the strap that secured the second, still-whimpering baby into the pushchair.

Michael held the first baby—Sophie?—at arm's length, totally at a loss as to what to do with her, and more than a little disconcerted to find himself the focus of eyes the same beautiful deep violet colour as her mother's. A steady and intense focus that seemed far too knowing, almost mocking it seemed to him, for a baby of surely only a few months old.

Eva lifted Sam up out of the pushchair as she straightened, more than a little annoyed that the two gabbling Archangel employees had woken the babies up at all; it had taken the whole of the walk from the hotel to the gallery to lull them into falling asleep in the first place, after a disjointed night of one or other of the twins—and consequently Eva—being woken up with teething pains.

As a result both Eva and the babies were feeling a little disgruntled this morning. Which didn't prevent her from almost laughing out loud as she turned to find D'Angelo was still holding Sophie with both arms straight out in front of him, a look of absolute horror on his face, as if the baby were a time bomb about to go off!

But Eva only almost laughed...

Because there had been very little for her to laugh about these past few nightmarish months.

Those memories sobered Eva instantly. 'Sophie doesn't bite,' she snapped impatiently as she cuddled a denim-and-T-shirt-clad Sam in her arms. 'Well...not much,' she amended ruefully. 'Luckily they both only have four teeth at the moment...'

Michael wasn't known for his patience at the best of times—and right now, in the midst of this chaos, was far from the best of times. 'I'm more interested in knowing what they, and you, are doing in the private area of Archangel, than in hearing how many teeth your children have!'

The woman's pointed chin rose as she looked at him with hard and challenging violet eyes. 'Do you really want me to discuss that in front of your employees, Mr D'Angelo? I take it that you are Mr D'Angelo?' She quirked a derisive brow.

'I am, yes.' Michael scowled darkly. 'Discuss what in front of my employees?' he prompted cautiously.

Her mouth thinned. 'The reason I'm in the private area of Archangel.'

He gave an impatient shake of his head. 'As I have absolutely no idea what your reasons might be I can't answer that question.'

'No?' she scorned.

'No,' Michael bit out harshly. 'Perhaps you would care to come through to my office...?'

Pierre, a man several years his junior, voiced his concern by launching into all the reasons—in French, of course!—as to why he felt it inadvisable for Michael to be alone with this woman, with several less than polite references made as to whether or not she was quite sane, along with the suggestion that they call security and have her ejected from the building.

'I understood all that,' their visitor answered in fluent French as she turned her glittering violet and challenging gaze on the now less than comfortable Pierre. 'And you can call security if you want, but, I assure you, I'm quite sane,' she mocked Michael.

'I never doubted it for a moment!' Michael drawled, equally mockingly. 'It's fine, Pierre,' he assured in English. 'If you would care to come through to my office…?' he prompted the woman again, before stepping out of the doorway to reveal the room behind him, still having no idea what to do with the baby in his arms. Especially as the baby—Sophie—was now smiling up at him beguilingly as she proudly displayed those four tiny white teeth.

'She likes you,' the baby's mother announced disgustedly as she continued to carry Sam at the same time as she manoeuvred the pushchair past Michael and into his office.

He hastily placed the piece of white linen on his shoulder and hefted the baby into one arm before he was able to close the office door behind him on the wide-eyed and slightly worried stares of Marie and Pierre.

'Wow, this is some view…'

Michael turned to see the violet-eyed woman gazing out of the floor-to-ceiling-windows at the view up the length of the Champs Élysées to the Arc de Triomphe; that view, and the prestigious address, were the main reasons for choosing this stunning location for the Paris gallery. 'We like it,' he drawled with hard dismissal. 'Now, if you wouldn't mind explaining yourself…?' he added pointedly. 'Beginning with who you are?' Michael had wondered briefly if she wasn't the persistent Monique from Rafe's past, but the English accent seemed to say not.

Eva turned, still holding a now-quiet Sam in her arms. 'My name is Eva Foster.'

'And?' D'Angelo prompted when she added nothing else to that statement, those obsidian-black eyes blank of emotion.

Eva eyed him impatiently. 'And you obviously have absolutely no idea who I am,' she realised with horror.

He arched dark brows. 'Should I have?'

Should he have? Of course he should, the arrogant, irresponsible jerk— 'Perhaps the name Rachel Foster would be more helpful in jogging your memory?' she prompted sweetly.

He frowned darkly even as he gave a slow shake of his head. 'I'm sorry, but I have absolutely no idea what—or who—you're talking about...'

A red tide seemed to pass in front of Eva's eyes. All these months of heartache, chaos, heartache, loss, and, yes, just plain heartache, and this man didn't even remember Rachel's name, let alone Rachel herself—!

'What sort of man are you? Don't bother to an-swer that,' Eva added furiously as she began to pace the office. 'Obviously so many women pass in and out of your privileged life, and your no doubt silk-sheeted bed, that you forget about them as soon as the next one takes up occupancy—'

'Stop right there,' D'Angelo advised harshly. 'No, I didn't mean you, little one,' he added softly as Sophie gave a protesting whimper at the tone of his voice. His eyes were as black and pierc-ing as jet as he turned back to Eva. 'Are you im-plying that you believe I've been…involved with this Rachel Foster?'

Eva's eyes widened angrily, her cheeks warm-ing with temper. 'This Rachel Foster happens to be my sister, and, yes, you've been "involved" with her. In fact, you're holding part of the ev-idence of that involvement in your arms right now!'

Michael instantly stared down at the baby he held. Not a newborn, certainly, probably a few months old, possibly five or six, and very cute, as babies went, with her mop of black hair, those violet-coloured eyes, and her little face screwed up in concentration as she played with one of the buttons on the jacket of his several-thousand-pound suit.

If this woman, this Eva Foster, was trying to say that he was somehow responsible?

Shades of yesterday...

'I've never met your sister,' Michael stated firmly. 'Let alone—I've never met her,' he repeated coldly. 'So whatever scam the two of you are trying to pull here I would advise that you forget it—' He broke off abruptly as one of Eva Foster's hands made loud and painful contact with one of his cheeks, causing the baby in his arms to let out another deafening wail. 'That was uncalled for,' he bit out between gritted teeth, his jaw clenched as he jiggled the baby up and down in his arms in an effort to silence her screams.

'It was very called for,' Eva Foster insisted heatedly, her face having become even paler as she moved forward to soothingly stroke the back of the baby in Michael's arms. 'How dare you stand there and deny even knowing my sister, accuse the two of us of trying to pull a scam on you, at the same time as you're holding your own daughter in your arms?' Her eyes flashed deeply violet in contrast to the emotional shaking of her voice.

'I am not—' Michael broke off to draw in a deep, controlling breath, his cheek still stinging from that slap. 'Sophie is not my daughter.'

'I assure you she is,' she snapped.

'Do you think we could both just take a couple of deep breaths, maybe step back a little, and try to calm this situation down? It's distressing the babies,' Michael added firmly as Eva Foster opened her mouth with the obvious intention of continuing to argue with him.

It was unusual for anyone to argue with him, period, Michael being accustomed to issuing orders and having them obeyed rather than have people dispute them. Nor did he appreciate the added complication of this woman—a feisty young woman he acknowledged as being irritatingly beautiful—continuing to accuse him of fathering her sister's babies.

It was an accusation Michael didn't appreciate. He'd learnt his lesson many years ago when it came to the machinations of women. And he had Emma Lowther to thank that, for teaching him to never, ever trust a woman, when it came to contraception or anything else.

How many years ago was it since Emma had

tried to blackmail him into marriage by claiming she was pregnant? Fourteen. And Michael still remembered every moment of it as if it were yesterday.

Not that he had ever thought of shirking his responsibility. Oh, no, Michael had been stupid enough to think he was actually in love with Emma, had even been pleased about the baby, and the two of them had been making wedding plans for weeks when he introduced Emma to an acquaintance at a party, and she had decided within days of that introduction that Daniel, his family richer even than Michael's, would be a far better choice as a husband. Which was when she had told Michael there was no baby, that she had been mistaken. Three months later she had tried to use the same trick on Daniel.

The scene that had followed, once Emma had learnt that Michael had warned Daniel of her machinations, that there was no baby this time either, had not been pleasant!

Emma's pregnancy had been a sham, a trick to make Michael marry her, and it had been enough of a warning for him never again to trust any woman to take care of contraception…

Which was why he could now confidently deny Eva Foster's claim in regard to her sister's babies.

'Twins,' she now corrected softly. 'The babies are twins.'

They certainly looked of a similar age and colouring: both had silky heads of ebony dark hair and the same amazing violet-coloured eyes as their aunt. Their features weren't completely formed as yet, but there were certainly enough similarities for Michael to accept Eva Foster's claim that they were twins.

But whether they were twins or otherwise, they were not—most definitely not!—Michael's children.

'How old are they?' he bit out tightly.

'Trying to jog your memory?' she scorned.

'How old?' Michael repeated through those gritted teeth.

She shrugged. 'Six months.'

And if Rachel Foster had gone full term with her babies that would mean nine months to be added onto the six months, making it fifteen months ago he was supposed to have—

Damn it, why was Michael even bothering to do the maths? No matter what this woman might claim to the contrary, he had not impregnated any woman fifteen months ago or at any other time!

'And you believe they're mine because…?' He kept his voice soft and even as Sophie's lids began to flicker and her head dropped down sleepily onto his shoulder, the infant obviously tired out by her previous screeching.

That pointed chin rose another challenging notch. 'Because Rachel told me they were.'

Michael nodded. 'In that case, would you care to explain why your sister hasn't come here and confronted me with this information herself?'

'Because— Careful!' Eva warned as she realised Sophie had fallen into the completely boneless sleep only babies seemed able to do, and was almost slipping off one of those broad shoulders as a result.

'How did you do that?' she breathed ruefully as she looked at the sleeping Sophie.

Usually the twins only fell asleep after she had walked them in their pushchair or bounced them up and down for hours; Eva couldn't remember the last time she'd had even one uninterrupted night's sleep. And those lazy Sunday mornings of dozing in bed until lunchtime, which she had once taken so much for granted, now seemed like a self-indulgent dream, a mirage, and one Eva was sure she was destined never to know again.

'Do what?' D'Angelo rasped softly.

'Never mind,' Eva muttered irritably. 'Just put Sophie in the left side of the pushchair. She doesn't like sitting on the right side,' she supplied wearily as he paused to raise dark, questioning brows.

'She's asleep, so what does it matter?'

'She knows when she wakes up,' Eva dismissed impatiently.

'Right,' Michael drawled dryly, willing to take this woman's word for it that a six-month-old baby was aware of which side of a pushchair she was sitting in.

He looked down at the baby after he had somehow managed to ease her down into the pushchair without waking her. Sophie was like a dark-haired angel, ebony lashes fanning across her flushed cheeks, her mouth a little pouting rosebud.

He straightened abruptly as he realised what he was doing. 'What about that one?' He indicated the baby in Eva Foster's arms.

'*His* name's Sam,' she supplied somewhat tartly. 'And he's just fine where he is.' She looked down indulgently at the baby now snuggled into her throat. 'Sam is more placid than Sophie,' she explained waspishly as she obviously saw Michael's mocking expression. 'What did you say?' she prompted softly as he muttered under his breath.

'I said that's probably because he's a man,' Michael repeated unabashedly.

Eva Foster gave a scathing snort. 'It's been my experience that men tend to be lazy, not placid!'

'I beg your pardon?' Michael's brow lowered.

'I'm sure you heard me the first time,' she came back with feigned sweetness.

He had, and he hadn't liked it either; he and his two brothers had worked damned hard the past ten years to develop the one gallery they had then owned into three, spread across London, New York and Paris, and to build them up to become some of the most prestigious private galleries and auction houses in the world. And the three brothers were now reaping some of the benefits of that hard work, all of them extremely wealthy and able to live a lifestyle befitting that wealth, then it certainly wasn't because it had just been handed to them on a silver platter.

The scornful expression on Eva Foster's delicately lovely face showed she obviously thought otherwise!

As she was also under some strange delusion that Michael was the father of her niece and nephew...

It was time—past time!—that he took control of this situation. 'In your opinion.' He nodded tersely as he moved to sit behind his black marble desk. 'You were about to tell me why you're here instead of your sister...?'

Eva was well aware of the fact that D'Angelo had deliberately chosen to resume his seat behind his desk, as a way of putting some distance between the two of them at the same time as it put their conversation onto a businesslike footing. Although how anyone could think, or talk, of babies in a 'businesslike' way was beyond her!

D'Angelo wasn't at all what she had been expecting of the man who had first charmed and then impregnated her younger sister. Rachel had been fun-loving, and, yes, slightly irresponsible, having decided to travel around the world for a year once she had finished university, only to come back to London ten months later, alone and pregnant. With this man's baby—which had turned out to be babies, plural.

The man seated behind the desk wasn't what Eva had imagined when her sister had talked so enthusiastically of her lover's charm and good looks, and the fun they'd had together in Paris. Oh, this man was certainly handsome enough, dark and brooding—dangerously so, she would hazard a guess, and causing Eva to give an inner wince as she looked at the mark her hand had left on one of those perfectly chiselled cheeks. No doubt that dangerous aura this man exuded was counteracted by the tight control he also showed, otherwise she might have found herself with a similar imprint on her own cheek!

His was such an austere handsomeness: icy black eyes, harshly etched features, his manner rigidly controlled, and there was a cool aloofness to him that it was difficult for Eva to imagine ever melting, even—especially!—when he made love with a woman.

She certainly couldn't imagine him and the

slightly irresponsible Rachel as ever having gone out together, let alone—

Maybe it would be better, for all concerned, if Eva's thoughts didn't dwell on the physical side of Rachel's relationship with this man. A physical relationship he continued to deny!

Her mouth thinned as she answered him. 'I'm here instead of Rachel because my sister is dead.'

He gave a visible start. 'What...?'

If Eva had thought to make him feel guilty, to get some reaction other than shock with the starkness of her statement, then she was disappointed; he looked suitably shocked, but in a distant way, rather than as a man hearing of the death of an ex-lover.

Eva drew in a sharp, shaky breath as she attempted to keep her own emotions under control. It was some weeks since she had needed to explain to anyone that her sister had died, and to do so now, to the man who had once been Rachel's lover—even if he denied all knowledge of it—was particularly hard.

Just as Eva still found it impossible to believe, to accept, that her sister Rachel, only twenty-two, and supposedly with all of her life still ahead of her, had died, quite peaceably in the end, just three short months ago.

And Eva had been trying to cope ever since with her own grief as well as the care of the twins. It was a battle she had finally had to accept she was losing, physically as well as financially. First Rachel had been so ill, and then she had died, and it had been—and still was—almost impossible for Eva to work when she had cared for Rachel and then had the full-time day-to-day care—and the sleepless nights—of the twins to cope with. Her savings had now dwindled almost to nothing, certainly quicker than she was able to replenish them with the few photographic assignments she had been free to accept these past six months. Assignments when she had been able to take the twins with her, which was becoming increasingly difficult the bigger and more vocal they got.

Which was why Eva had decided, rather than giving D'Angelo the opportunity to fob her off in a telephone call, to instead use the last of her savings to fly herself and the twins over to Paris yesterday, so that she might confront the babies' father face to face with his responsibilities.

Much as Eva might hate having to do it, after much soul-searching, she knew she no longer had any choice but to try and seek D'Angelo's help from a financial point of view, at least, for the good of the twins.

Michael stood up abruptly as he saw how pale Eva Foster's face had become, adding to that air of fragility. Her sister's death, caring for the twins, went some way to explaining those dark shadows beneath those beautiful violet-coloured eyes.

He crossed economically to the drinks cabinet in the seating area of his office to look at the array of bottles, deciding against offering her alcohol and instead choosing to bring her a bottle of water from the small fridge. He very much doubted Eva Foster would have accepted drinking a more reviving whisky, when she had two young babies in her care.

'Here, let me take Sam, while you sit down over here,' he rasped abruptly as he saw Eva Foster was swaying slightly on her canvas-shod feet. Not waiting for her reply, he took the baby from her unresisting arms before placing his free hand lightly beneath her elbow to guide her over to the seating area and eased her down onto the black leather sofa.

'Sorry about that,' Eva murmured shakily after taking a much-needed sip of the ice-cold water. It was very warm outside, and it had been a long walk to the Archangel gallery from the cheap hotel she had booked into with the twins yesterday. 'I think I'm doing okay and then suddenly the grief just hits me again when I'm least expecting it.'

Although she should have realised that this meeting with Rachel's lover was going to be far from easy. Just as coming to Paris at all, seeking out D'Angelo, hadn't been an easy decision for her to make in the first place. In Eva's eyes, it almost smacked of defeat.

But she'd had no other choice, she assured herself determinedly; this was for the twins' benefit, not hers. As it was, she would far rather spit in this man's eye than so much as have to speak to him, let alone ask him for help!

'I'm sorry for your loss,' D'Angelo murmured gruffly.

Was he? Considering he had denied all knowledge of Rachel just minutes ago, Eva found that a little hard to believe!

She still couldn't quite come to terms with Rachel ever having been involved with this austerely cold man at all; Rachel had been outgoing and warm in nature, and this man was anything but. But maybe it had been a case of opposites attracting? D'Angelo was certainly attractive enough, and he possessed an inborn confidence, an arrogance, that Rachel might have found attractive, even challenging. This man's controlled aloofness would represent a challenge to any red-blooded female.

Even Eva?

The last thing she wanted was to find the man who had fathered the twins in the least attractive!

Eva sat forward to place the bottle of water on the coffee table in front of her. 'I think you can put him down too now...' she drawled ruefully as she realised that Sam—the traitor!—had also fallen asleep on one of D'Angelo's broad and muscled shoulders. All those hours of pacing and walking, a twin on each of her shoulders, and D'Angelo just had to hold them to have the twins instantly fall asleep!

Because they instinctively recognised who he was? Maybe. As Eva had learnt these past few months, babies were far more intuitive than she had ever realised; the twins had both certainly quickly picked up on Eva's own nervousness in caring for them twenty-four seven, making a battle of their first few weeks together.

Michael turned to look at Eva Foster after he had secured the sleeping Sam in the pushchair beside his sister, relieved to see that, although the shadows beneath her eyes remained, those porcelain cheeks had at least regained a little of their colour, that pallor having been emphasised by straight and glossy ebony hair to just below her shoulders.

He was more than a little troubled himself to learn of the death of this woman's sister, the mother of the sleeping babies. 'How old was she…?'

Eva Foster looked at him blankly. 'Who?'

'Your sister Rachel.'

Derisive brows rose over those violet-coloured eyes. 'The two of you were too busy to discuss ages?'

Michael drew in a sharp breath at the obvious

derision in her tone. 'I repeat that, to my knowl-edge, I didn't so much as even meet your sister in order to be able to discuss our respective ages, let alone father her twins!'

'And I repeat, I don't believe you,' Eva Foster stated coldly.

'I can see that.' Michael nodded grimly.

She drew in a shaky breath. 'Rachel was just twenty-two when she died, three years younger than me,' she stated huskily.

'In childbirth?'

'No.' She grimaced. 'They discovered, during a routine scan partway through the pregnancy, that Rachel had a tumour.'

'God!'

Eva Foster nodded abruptly. 'Rachel refused to have the pregnancy terminated, or to have treat-ment for the tumour, because of the danger of harming the babies. She...died when they were three months old.' And the pain of that loss, of the consequences of her sister's decision, was now etched into that creamy brow and in the lines of strain beside those violet eyes and sensuously sculptured mouth...

'What about your parents...?' he prompted huskily.

'They both died in a car crash eighteen months ago.'

Michael folded his lean length down into the armchair opposite the sofa, uncomfortable towering over Eva Foster in the circumstances, at the same time as he recognised she wouldn't appreciate him sitting down beside her on the sofa. There was currently a defensive aura about Eva Foster, an invisible barrier that was preventing her from breaking down completely.

Not surprising, when first her parents had died and she had now lost her younger sister so tragically. Michael was the eldest of the three D'Angelo brothers, and he couldn't imagine— didn't want to imagine—the devastation he would feel if he should ever lose his parents so suddenly, or Gabriel or Rafe before they had all grown old and grey together.

Which still didn't change the fact that he had absolutely no knowledge of Rachel Foster, or her babies. 'Where did Rachel and the babies' father meet?' he prompted gruffly.

Eva Foster shot him an impatient glance. 'Right here in the gallery.'

Michael did some mental arithmetic. 'I wasn't in Paris, or the gallery here, fifteen months ago.'

'What…?' Eva looked at him blankly.

He grimaced. 'I wasn't in Paris fifteen months ago, Eva,' he repeated gently. 'Until recently, my brothers and I have moved around the three galleries on a rotation basis,' he added as she still stared at him dazedly. 'I was at the New York gallery fifteen months ago, organising a gala exhibition of Mayan art.'

She gave a slow shake of her head. 'I don't— My sister said—'

'Yes?'

Eva could barely breathe, a sinking, nauseous sensation in the pit of her stomach as she prompted warily, 'Exactly who are you…?'

He gave a tight smile. 'Isn't it a little late to be asking me that when you've already accused me of having been "involved" with your sister and fathering your niece and nephew?'

Eva's mouth had gone so dry she didn't even have enough saliva left to moisten the stiffness of her equally dry lips. 'I assumed— Who are you?'

she demanded to know shakily, her hands tightly clenched together as they rested on her thighs.

'Michael D'Angelo.'

*Michae*l D'Angelo? *Michael* not—

Eva thought she might actually be physically sick at the realisation that all this time she had been accusing the *wrong* D'Angelo brother of fathering the twins!

CHAPTER TWO

OH, GOOD GRIEF, why hadn't Eva thought to ask this man for his full name? To find out which of the D'Angelo brothers she was actually talking to before—before—well, at least before she had launched into her accusations?

Unfortunately, Eva knew exactly why she hadn't done any of those things…

Because this man—Michael D'Angelo—brought out a response in her, a physical awareness, she had considered as being entirely inappropriate in regard to the man she had believed to have been involved with Rachel.

Not that it was any less inappropriate now; he was still the *brother* of the man who had fathered the twins!

He was just so much larger than life, exuded a confidence, an aura of power, that caused Eva to be aware of everything about him: the way his hair was inclined to curl slightly at his ears and nape, the intensity of those black-on-black eyes, the harsh and yet somehow mesmerising sensual lines of his finely sculptured face, and as for the way his shoulders and chest filled out his perfectly tailored jacket, and the slim cut of his trousers emphasised the lean length of his long legs—

'Drink some more water.' Michael was suddenly down on his haunches beside Eva holding out the water bottle towards her.

Eva took the bottle with shaking fingers, drinking thirstily as she realised she was starting to hyperventilate just thinking about the way this man looked. At the same time she inwardly cringed as she recalled all of their conversation, the things she had said, the accusations she had made—and all *to the wrong man*!

His identity as *Michael* D'Angelo certainly explained why Eva hadn't been able to imagine her fun-loving sister Rachel ever being attracted to such a coldly aloof man who was also so much older than her, let alone involved in the passionate affair with him that had resulted in the birth of the twins!

None of which helped the awkwardness of the

situation Eva now found herself in. 'It seems I owe you an apology,' she murmured stiffly. 'I— Obviously I made a mistake. I— It— I don't know what else to say…' She groaned self-consciously, unable to look Michael D'Angelo in the eye now.

Unable to look into that coolly arrogant face at all. A face, a man, she shouldn't find in the least attractive.

Except Eva knew that she did…

She couldn't stop herself from giving him a brief sideways glance, once again struck by the chiselled perfection of Michael D'Angelo's features: those black obsidian eyes that revealed so little of the man's thoughts or feelings, those sculptured cheekbones, his mouth—dear Lord, this man's mouth was pure perfection, the top lip fuller than the bottom.

Possibly as an indication he had a deeply sensual nature?

If it was, then Eva was sure it was a sensuality this coldly aloof man always kept firmly under his own iron control!

This man…

Michael D'Angelo.

A man Eva knew she had to guard herself against being any more attracted to.

He straightened abruptly. 'As I said earlier, maybe we should both take a few deep breaths, a step back, and calm this situation down?'

Eva still felt as if she was on the edge of hyperventilating again rather than calming down!

Having made the hard decision to come to Paris in the first place, she had planned out in her mind exactly how her meeting with D'Angelo was going to proceed once she arrived here.

She would find a way to confront D'Angelo.

Which she had done.

He would deny any and all involvement with Rachel.

Which he had done.

Eva would then scorn that denial, with the twins as proof of that 'involvement'.

Which she had done.

D'Angelo's accusation that she and Rachel were trying to pull some sort of scam on him, by claiming the babies were his, had been unexpected...

As much as Eva's response, slapping his face,

had been; she had never thought of herself as being a person capable of violence until today!

And the conversation had seemed to go downhill from there…

She drew in several deep and steadying breaths before speaking again, determined not to lose complete control of this situation.

'That's all well and good, Mr D'Angelo, but I think you're still missing the point here.'

Michael D'Angelo quirked one dark and arrogant brow. 'Which is?'

Eva straightened her shoulders determinedly as she met his gaze unblinkingly. 'That you may be correct in claiming not to be the twins' father—'

'I assure you, I am not their father,' he bit out hardly.

'—but that doesn't change the fact that one of your brothers most certainly is,' Eva continued firmly, her gaze meeting his challengingly now.

At the same time, she inwardly questioned just how Michael D'Angelo could speak so certainly of never having fathered a baby by Rachel. Eva certainly didn't believe it was from physically abstaining. Beneath this man's aloofness she sensed that sensuality, deep and dark, an indication that, once aroused, he would be the type of lover who would demand and possess a woman completely.

He was also, Eva acknowledged with a frown, a man who would need to be in control at all times, and as such he would no doubt ensure that he would never forget to take the necessary precautions to ensure that no unwanted pregnancy ensued from any of his relationships with women.

Something Eva should probably have realised *before* she accused him of being the twins' father!

Michael's breath left him in a hiss as he took in the full ramifications of Eva Foster's revelations. Almost wishing now—almost!—that he *had* been the one responsible for fathering Rachel Foster's twin babies. Because for either of his younger brothers to be the father—his now both very much married younger brothers—would be a disaster of unthinkable proportions.

Not that Gabriel or Rafe had been married fifteen months ago, when the twins were conceived, but they were now, Gabriel for just five weeks, Rafe for only a matter of days. And it would surely be asking a lot—too much, perhaps—for either Bryn or Nina to accept that either of their respective husbands had fathered the now six-month-old twins with another woman!

His mouth thinned. 'I think, having already made one mistake, that you need to be a little more certain of your facts before you go around making any more accusations.'

Colour warmed Eva Foster's porcelain cheeks. 'My mistake—for which I've apologised—' she added uncomfortably, 'doesn't alter the fact that one of your brothers fathered Sophie and Sam.'

Michael turned away to give himself the privacy for the emotions he was sure must be apparent on his face: dismay, concern, and not a little anger, all of them directed towards whichever of his brothers had caused this current situation.

He thrust his hands in the pockets of his trousers as he walked over to stand in front of the windows, for once totally blind to the magnificent view outside. Because he could never remember feeling quite so helpless, so out of his depth with a situation. Until now.

As the eldest brother, even if only by a year and two years respectively, he had always been protective of Rafe and Gabriel—sometimes too much so for their liking. But in this present situation—surely a disaster just waiting to happen, no matter which of his brothers Eva Foster was accusing?—he couldn't think of any way in which to avert the coming disaster.

But for which one of his brothers…?

The outwardly light-hearted but inwardly determined and assertive Rafe, who had finally found, fallen in love with and married the beautiful Nina, the perfect woman to counterbalance those apparent contradictions in his mercurial nature?

Or Gabriel, in love with Bryn for the past five years but thinking it an impossible love, a lost love, that he had no right to, only for the two of them to meet again and learn that it wasn't, now happily married to each other?

Whichever of his brothers was responsible it was sure to cause—

'Rafe.'

Michael's eyes were narrowed as he turned sharply back to face Eva Foster. 'What?' he rasped harshly, coldly, already knowing what her answer was going to be but wishing—so much wishing—that he didn't.

'It was Rafe that Rachel was involved with fifteen months ago,' Eva Foster supplied abruptly.

Michael had already worked out in his mind which of his two brothers had been in charge of the Paris gallery fifteen months ago, and it now took tremendous effort of will on his part to keep his expression remote and unemotional as Eva Foster confirmed his worst fear.

Oh, Michael had no doubt that Nina loved Rafe unconditionally, and that his brother loved Nina in the same way, and that somehow, between the two of them, they would find a way to deal with this situation, for their marriage to survive the blow.

But Nina's father, the rich and powerful Dmitri Palitov, was another matter entirely. His protection of his daughter was absolute, and he would not look kindly on anyone who dared to threaten Nina's happiness.

Michael knew that Rafe was more than capable of taking care of himself; it was Eva Foster for whom he now felt concern...

'I hope you'll forgive me if I'm still a little sceptical as to the accuracy of your accusation!' Michael now rasped scathingly.

While inwardly his heart was beating errati-
cally, and his thoughts racing, as he tried to think
of some way to come up with some proof that
Eva Foster was wrong for the second time in regard to the identity of the twins' father.

Except…

Until Rafe met and fell in love with Nina, he
had played fast and loose with dozens of beautiful women—something Michael had warned
him about on more than one occasion.

And there was no changing the fact that Rafe
had been here at the Paris Archangel fifteen
months ago.

Most importantly of all—despite her initial
mistake in having thought Michael was Rafe—
Eva Foster seemed very certain of the name of
the man responsible for having fathered her niece
and nephew…

'Be as sceptical as you like,' she came back
evenly. 'We'll both know the truth once I've had
a chance to speak to your brother.'

That was what Michael was afraid of! 'Obviously he isn't in Paris at the moment.'

'I suppose you're now going to tell me that I
need not have put myself through the trauma of

flying to Paris with the twins,' she drawled self-derisively, 'because Rafe is currently at the London Archangel gallery?'

Michael was having trouble speaking at all, his thoughts were so chaotic. Unusual for him, but then this situation was beyond anything he'd ever had to deal with before.

One thing he was sure of, and that was that he didn't want Eva Foster roaming about, here or in London, repeating her accusations to anyone else. Not till he'd had the chance to talk to Rafe. Something Michael had no intention of doing for the next two weeks, at least!

'No.' He spoke softly. 'I'm not going to tell you that.'

'Please don't tell me he's at the New York gallery!' Eva groaned. She couldn't bear even the thought of flying all the way to New York with six-month-old twins who were cranky most of the time because they were both teething. Although to look at the two of them now, both sleeping like little angels, no one would ever believe it!

'No, I'm not going to tell you that, either...' Michael D'Angelo answered slowly.

Eva looked at him between narrowed lids, finding it impossible to read anything from his closed expression; those black-on-black eyes were completely without emotion, the harshness of his features set into hard, uncompromising lines. 'And we've already established he isn't here, either, so where is he?' she prompted suspiciously.

'Unavailable.'

Her brows rose at the terseness of Michael D'Angelo's answer. 'That isn't an acceptable answer, I'm afraid.'

His mouth tightened grimly. 'It's the only one you're going to get for the moment.'

Eva eyed him shrewdly. 'Why "for the moment"…?' she finally prompted guardedly.

This woman was too astute for her own good, Michael recognised impatiently. For his good too. And most certainly for Rafe's!

'It just isn't,' Michael bit out between clenched teeth.

Obviously this woman hadn't seen the photographs in the Sunday newspapers of Rafe and Nina's marriage on Saturday, no doubt because caring for six-month-old twins didn't leave her a lot of time for doing anything else. But Michael knew that he couldn't keep that truth from her indefinitely.

Eva Foster bristled. 'I need to speak to him urgently.'

He nodded. 'Anything you have to say to Rafe you can say to me.'

'Having already made that mistake once, I don't think so!' she bit out.

Michael's nostrils flared his impatience. 'I will naturally pass on your…concerns, to my brother, when I next speak to him, but other than that—'

'No,' Eva Foster stated firmly as she stood up abruptly. 'That simply isn't good enough, Mr D'Angelo,' she answered his questioningly raised brows. 'I need to talk to him now,' she insisted, 'not after you next happen to speak to him.'

Michael had to give this woman credit for tenacity—all five feet and a dot of her!

That determined glitter in those violet-coloured eyes said she wasn't about to back down any time soon either, not from him, or her demand that she speak to Rafe. 'I've already said that isn't possible.'

Her eyes flashed. 'Then I suggest you *make* it possible, Mr D'Angelo!'

'I don't care for your tone,' he bit out harshly.

Eva shrugged. 'Then maybe you should stop trying to prevent me from speaking with your brother.'

Michael bit back his own anger. 'The twins are now six months old, so why this sudden urgency to speak to the man your sister told you was their father?'

'He is their father,' Eva insisted stubbornly.

And why the sudden urgency…? Because Eva, much as she had tried, much as she hated having to admit defeat, knew that she just couldn't cope any more without help. Financially. Or emotionally.

Although she had no intention of admitting the latter to the aloofly controlled and ultra-self-confident Michael D'Angelo, a man who looked capable of dealing with any situation…

How could a man like him possibly understand the crippling heartache that washed over Eva like a dark and oppressive tide whenever she allowed herself to dwell on the death of her sister Rachel, let alone how inadequate Eva felt, no matter how much she might love the twins, for the task of caring for two rapidly growing babies?

And all of that was apart from the fact that she simply didn't have enough money coming in to be able to afford the care the twins needed now, or in the future.

There was no way Eva could go away on photographic assignments any more, because she simply couldn't leave the twins for any length of time. Even taking local assignments, going back to the well-paid but monotonous photography of weddings and christenings was becoming problematic as the twins grew older, making it increasingly difficult for Eva to take them with her; brides tended to frown at having the photographer's twin babies scream at their wedding!

And even if Eva could manage to find a childminder that she trusted it was going to cost yet more money, and so eat into any of the fees she might earn from her work.

No, Eva had thought long and hard before seeking out Rafe D'Angelo, considered her options carefully, and, unpalatable as this alternative might be, she couldn't see any other way out of this problem other than asking the twins' father for financial help.

It wasn't as if she wanted anything else from

him, just a way of being able to care for the twins without having to worry where the next penny was coming from. But that was all she wanted.

After meeting and speaking with Michael D'Angelo, Eva was convinced the less physical interaction any of the D'Angelo family had with the twins—and her!—the better she would like it!

She gave a shake of her head. 'It's your brother Rafe I need to speak to, Mr D'Angelo, not you.'

Michael had no idea as to the thoughts that had been going through Eva Foster's head these past few moments, but he did know they hadn't been pleasant ones. Her face was once again as pale as bone china, those deep shadows under her violet-coloured eyes more prominent, and the fullness of her mouth appeared to be trembling slightly, as further evidence of her vulnerability.

An air of vulnerability Michael had a feeling this woman would hate intensely if she was made aware of it!

He narrowed his eyes. 'Have you eaten any-thing today?'

She gave him a startled look at this sudden change of subject. 'Sorry?'

He shrugged. 'It's almost lunchtime, and you're looking a little pale, so I wondered if you had eaten anything today.'

She blinked long sooty lashes. 'I— Yes, I believe I did manage to grab a piece of toast while I was feeding the twins their breakfast.'

No doubt she only managed to grab something to eat a lot of the time with two small babies to care for! 'At your hotel?'

She gave a slightly derisive smile. 'I believe you would call it more of a *pension* than a hotel. It was the best I could afford, okay?' she added defensively as Michael's frown deepened. 'We can't all live in penthouse apartments in major cities around the world and fly about in private jets, you know!'

There was no denying that Michael did exactly that, as did his two brothers. Which was no doubt one of the reasons Eva Foster had decided to seek out the twins' father and ask for his help... 'And where is this pension?'

'It's in a back street just a short walk away from the Gare du Nord,' she revealed reluctantly. 'Look, if I could just speak to your brother—'

'I take it you intend to ask him for financial help when you do speak with him?'

Her cheeks flushed. 'It's my intention to remind him of his financial responsibility towards his two children, yes— Don't look at me like that!' she snapped sharply, her slender hands clenched so tightly together her knuckles showed white.

'How am I looking at you?' Michael prompted evenly.

'As if you still think I'm some sort of gold-digger out to fleece your brother out of some of his millions!' She gave a disgusted shake of her head. 'It wasn't easy for me to come here, you know.' She began to pace the office restlessly. 'The last thing I want is any contact with the twins' obviously reluctant father—'

'Are you saying that Rafe knows of the twins' existence…?' Michael looked at her through narrowed lids. If his brother had known of Rachel Foster's pregnancy and not told him, or, more importantly, not told Nina…!

Eva Foster came to an abrupt halt. 'I— No. I don't think so.'

'But you aren't sure?'

'Not absolutely, no.' Eva grimaced. 'But I'm assuming not. Rachel wasn't exactly forthcoming on the subject, except to tell me the name of her lover, and that the relationship was over by the time she found out she was pregnant,' she added heavily. 'I was out of the country when Rachel first realised she was pregnant, and she never so much as mentioned it during our weekly telephone conversations. By the time I returned to England she was already five months pregnant and had been diagnosed with the cancer.' She sighed. 'Pressing Rachel for more details of the babies' father, other than to tell me his name before she died, didn't seem very important at the time.'

'I imagine not.' Michael nodded. 'Returned from where?' For some reason he found himself more than a little interested as to why Eva Foster should have been out of her native England for several months.

She frowned. 'Does that matter?'

He shrugged. 'Just filling in the details.'

Eva shot him an irritated glare, sure that this man wasn't usually a man who cared for 'details', that he usually left such trivia for other people to deal with; he commanded, others obeyed! 'My work often takes me out of England. At least, it did,' she added with a grimace.

'Rachel was so ill the last six months of her life, and since then I've been caring for the twins on my own.'

'You haven't been able to work since your sister died?'

'Not properly, no.' It was the truth, so what else could she say?

'What—?'

'Look, my career, my life, none of this is up for discussion,' she snapped irritably.

She loved the twins, adored them actually, not just for themselves, but because they were all she had left of Rachel.

But Eva had trained and worked hard to become successful in a career that was dominated by men, and these past nine months of being unable to do that career had taken their toll, on both Eva personally, and the respect she had worked so hard to achieve for her photography.

'I disagree,' Michael D'Angelo bit out coolly. 'If—and it's still a big if, as far as I'm concerned—' he warned hardly, 'it should transpire that Rafe is the twins' father, then your career, and your life, would certainly both be very much up for discussion.'

Eva stilled as she looked across at him searchingly, a panicked fluttering beginning in her chest as she saw the hard, uncompromising jet of his eyes and the grim set of those sculptured lips.

She gave a slow, guarded shake of her head. 'Rachel made me the twins' legal guardian before she died...'

Dark brows rose. 'And their biological father would naturally take precedence over their maternal aunt.'

That panicked flutter turned into a full surge as Eva's heart seemed to be squeezed tightly inside her chest. 'Are you threatening to take the twins away from me, Mr D'Angelo...?'

Whatever it was Michael was doing, he certainly wasn't deriving any pleasure out of it. Inwardly he felt as if he were kicking an already starved and abused kitten.

Although this particular starved and abused kitten would probably spit in his eye as soon as look at him...

CHAPTER THREE

MICHAEL KNEW THE reputation he had, that most people believed him to be both cold and ruthless, an automaton without a heart, and in business perhaps that accusation was true. And no doubt many of his past lovers would also agree with that sentiment; several of the women he had been involved with over the years had accused him of lacking that particular organ when he had ended their relationship!

But Michael loved his family dearly—his parents and his two brothers, and now their two wives—and he would do anything he had to do in order to protect each and every one of them.

Even to the extent of browbeating a young, defenceless woman who only wanted to do what she believed was right for the only family she had left, namely her orphaned niece and nephew?

Unfortunately, yes.

But only because Michael didn't feel he had

any choice. Because he dared not allow Eva Foster to repeat this wild accusation to anyone else until he'd had a chance to speak with Rafe, and he wasn't going to do that until Rafe and Nina returned from their honeymoon. And if the only way to achieve Eva Foster's silence was to put the fear of God into her, by giving her the impression that Rafe, if he should be the twins' father, might want custody of them, then that was what he'd do.

His brother was headstrong, yes, had deliberately earned himself the reputation of being something of a playboy these past fifteen years, but falling in love with Nina had changed his need for that armour. They were two very small, adorable babies, Michael acknowledged as he looked down at the angelically sleeping twins. The truth was Michael had absolutely no idea how Rafe would react to knowing, if it were true, that he had fathered twins with a woman other than Nina.

Michael only knew how he would feel in the same situation!

No matter what the cost to himself, to any other relationship he might have in his life at the time, Michael knew he would want his children with him. And Rafe, despite the outward differences in their personalities, was enough like him to feel the same way. Which was the reason Michael, at least, was convinced Rachel Foster hadn't told Rafe anything about her pregnancy or the twins' birth.

'I'm merely stating a fact, Miss Foster,' Michael answered her abruptly. 'Not that I'm saying that would definitely be the case, only that you should consider it as a possibility.'

Eva didn't want to even consider the idea of the twins ever being taken away from her!

Yes, she found it difficult, all-consuming, to care for two small babies night and day, but she would dare any woman in the same situation, even the natural mother, to deny that it was hard work.

And yes, caring for the twins had also put her career on semi-permanent hold.

But that didn't mean she would ever willingly give them up.

The opposite, in fact; she knew she would fight tooth and nail to prevent that from ever happening.

She strode over to take control of the babies' pushchair. 'Perhaps I made a mistake coming here.'

'I'm afraid it's too late for that, Eva.'

She stilled, as much at hearing Michael D'Angelo speak her name in that husky, nerve-tingling tone as at the words he had spoken.

And how stupid of her was that?

Michael D'Angelo was too arrogantly handsome for his own good, wealthy beyond belief, extremely powerful—worse, he was using those last two things to threaten her—and her only response was to once again feel that quiver of awareness down the length of her spine, to feel her breasts swelling beneath her T-shirt, and the nipples tightening, engorging, in physical arousal.

More humiliating still, they were no doubt engorged nipples that Michael D'Angelo would be able to see pressing against the tightness of her T-shirt!

Eva couldn't quite meet the darkness of his gaze as she gave him an over-bright smile at the same time as she turned the pushchair towards the office door. 'I'm sure I've taken up enough of your valuable time for one day, Mr D'Angelo—'

'You aren't leaving, Eva.'

She gave him a startled glance as she came to an abrupt halt. 'What do you mean? Of course I'm leaving.'

'This office, maybe—'

'There's no "maybe" about it—'

'—but I'm afraid I can't allow you to leave Paris until I've spoken to Rafe,' Michael D'Angelo continued as if she hadn't spoken, the authority in his voice unmistakeable, despite the even softness of his tone.

'You can't *allow* me!' Eva stared at him incredulously. 'Forgive me, Mr D'Angelo, but at what point in this conversation did you think I gave you the right to tell me what I can or can't do?'

He gave a tight smile. 'I believe, Miss Foster, that it was at the point you told me it's your belief that my brother Rafe is the father of your niece and nephew.'

Eva's eyes narrowed. 'I think that's for Rafe and me to discuss further, don't you?'

'And that's where the problem lies.'

'I still fail to see why…?'

Michael drew in a deep controlling breath, hating what he was doing, but knowing he had no real choice. The fact that Eva Foster was so far unaware of Rafe's recent marriage didn't mean that she would remain so, and for Rafe and Nina's sake Michael had no choice but to keep an eye—a very close eye—on the young woman who could put a serious strain on his brother's recent marriage. And for Michael to be able to do that Eva Foster had to remain in Paris...

His mouth thinned. 'I've already told you my brother isn't available for either of us to talk to right now—'

'And very mysterious you were about it, if you want my opinion!' Those violet-coloured eyes snapped with temper. 'Which you probably don't,' she added scathingly as he continued to look at her coolly. 'I have the distinct impression you don't care for anyone else's opinion but your own!'

'I don't believe resorting to insults to be in the least constructive to this situation, Miss Foster,' he bit out icily.

'It's making *me* feel better,' Eva came back tartly.

Michael D'Angelo raised dark brows. 'And why is that?'

Why was that? Because the power this man exuded unnerved her. Just as his dark and charismatic good looks unsettled her. Worst of all, she found her physical reaction to him deeply disturbing.

And Eva didn't want to be unnerved, unsettled, or disturbed. She had realised, after this single meeting with Michael D'Angelo, that she would need to keep all of her wits about her when dealing with any of the D'Angelo family.

'You threatened me a few minutes ago,' she reminded tautly.

'I asked that you remain in Paris until Rafe returns.'

'As I remember it you didn't ask, you ordered,' Eva corrected dryly. 'And exactly where in the world is your brother Rafe that you can't just pick up a mobile phone and speak to him right here and right now?'

Michael D'Angelo sighed, his expression grim. 'It isn't the where he is, it's the why.'

'Why what?' Eva was completely puzzled by Michael D'Angelo's evasive behaviour; he didn't seem like the sort of man who would feel the need to avoid any situation.

'Why I consider Rafe to be currently unreachable as well as unavailable,' he revealed tightly.

'And are you going to tell me what that "why" is…?'

'It would seem I have little choice in the matter, when you could pick up any newspaper or simply go online and find out for yourself!' he bit out with exasperated impatience.

'You're starting to alarm me…' Eva frowned uncertainly.

'That wasn't my intention.' Michael sighed his frustration with this situation.

His day had started out like any other, the alarm going off at seven o'clock, allowing him time to shower and dress before leaving his apartment to walk to his favourite coffee shop, to sit down at his usual table and enjoy two cups of their strong coffee with delicious buttery croissants, before then strolling further along the street at eight-thirty to enter Archangel, and begin his day's work.

At no time in the past four hours had Michael had so much as a single indication that his day, his week—his year!—was going to be shot down in flames by a tiny violet-eyed firebrand and her baby niece and nephew!

But it had been, it still was, and would continue to be so until so he had a chance to speak with Rafe, so for the moment he had no choice but to deal with this situation as best he could...

Eva felt a sinking sensation in the pit of her stomach as Michael D'Angelo lifted his arrogantly chiselled chin to look at her with those glittering onyx-black eyes, telling Eva that whatever he was about to say to her she wasn't going to like it!

His jaw tightened. 'Rafe was married two days ago and is currently away on his honeymoon.'

Eva felt herself pale even as she reached out to grasp the back of one of the leather armchairs in an effort to stop herself from collapsing completely, her knees having gone weak, a loud buzzing sound inside her head.

'Here, sit down in this chair!'

Eva barely heard Michael D'Angelo's rasped instruction over the increased buzzing inside her head, offering no resistance as he took a light grasp of her arm to ease her down into one of the leather armchairs before straightening to step back and away from her, seeming to realise that she needed time and space in which to deal with her turmoil of thoughts.

Not that any amount of time or space was going to make this situation seem less disastrous!

Rafe D'Angelo was now married.

Worse than that, he had only been married for two days.

Just forty-eight hours!

If Eva had sought him out just a week ago, even three days ago, then it might have been different, but as things stood this now seemed like an impossible situation. It was one thing to approach Rafe D'Angelo and ask for his financial help with the twins, something else completely for Eve to possibly wreck his marriage before it had even begun.

Despite Eva's urgings for her to do so, Rachel hadn't really wanted to talk about Rafe D'Angelo after revealing the name of her babies' father. As far as her sister was concerned it had been a holiday romance, the two of them not in love with each other, just enjoying a couple of weeks' fun together in Paris.

Rachel had been totally realistic about the

whole affair. It had happened, and it was over when she left Paris, and that was the end of the relationship as far as she was concerned. Learning of her pregnancy hadn't changed Rachel's mind about that in the slightest.

The decision to now seek out Rafe D'Angelo, to ask for his financial help with the twins, at least, had been completely Eva's own idea.

And she couldn't have chosen a worse time to do it!

Much as Eva needed Rafe D'Angelo's help with the twins, she wasn't a vindictive person, was well aware of the chaos it would cause if she was to force her way into his life now, with the twins in tow. As for his poor wife—!

Eva tried to imagine how she would feel if confronted with twin babies belonging to her new husband. Oh, God…!

No wonder Michael D'Angelo had been so adamant that neither he nor Eva could talk to Rafe 'right here and now'. He could hardly contact his brother on his *honeymoon* and tell him of Eva's presence in Paris, along with his son and daughter!

She drew in a deep breath, her head clearing

slightly as she did so, willing her pulse to slow as she looked up at the broodingly silent Michael D'Angelo. 'I couldn't have come here at a worse time.' It was a statement rather than a question.

'Oh, I don't know,' he drawled dryly. 'I have a feeling that four o'clock in New York on Saturday would have been an even less welcome time for you to break the news. Rafe and Nina were married there at three o'clock,' he explained in response to Eva's puzzled frown.

And she didn't appreciate it if that was supposed to be Michael D'Angelo's attempt at humour—from a man who looked as if he very rarely found anything to smile about! 'What do I do now?' She gave a slightly dazed shake of her head.

'What do *we* do now?' Michael corrected hardly.

As far as he was concerned his decision not to let Eva Foster roam around Paris or London like a loose cannon, and in the process possibly arouse people's curiosity as to her reason for doing so, still stood. Marie and Pierre's obvious curiosity about her earlier was an example of exactly how that could, and no doubt would, occur!

No, until it became possible for Michael to talk

to Rafe he intended keeping Eva Foster, and these two babies, well away from the public and curious eye. At great inconvenience to himself, he might add. Rafe had better appreciate what he was doing for him, because Michael had no doubt the next couple of weeks were going to be excruciatingly painful ones for him. His brother was certainly going to owe him—big time!

'I don't understand...' Eva Foster looked up at him blankly, obviously still suffering under some degree of shock at learning of Rafe's recent marriage.

Michael grimaced. 'How long did you intend staying in Paris...?'

She blinked. 'My return flight is booked for three days' time—I didn't think it would take more than a day or two to speak with your brother,' she added defensively as Michael frowned.

'Cutting it a little fine, weren't you?' he rasped impatiently. 'Never mind, we can cancel that flight and—'

'I have no intention of cancelling my flight.' Eva stood up abruptly. 'Coming here at all was a risk, and I have even less reason to stay on in

Paris now that I know your brother isn't even here.' Or likely to be available anywhere any time soon for her to be able to talk to him, when he was currently on his *honeymoon*!

She should have telephoned before coming to Paris, of course, at least established that Rafe D'Angelo was actually in the city before flying over here and coming to the Archangel gallery and insisting on seeing him.

That was what Eva should have done. Except she hadn't wanted to alert the man to her imminent arrival, had hoped to catch him off guard, preventing him from leaving Paris before she had even arrived.

And instead Rafe was away on his honeymoon and she was faced with Michael D'Angelo in his stead. A man who Eva already knew she had to guard herself against becoming any more disturbed than she cared to think about!

Michael D'Angelo now narrowed those piercing black-on-black eyes. 'You have some reason for hurrying back to London, perhaps? A boyfriend? Live-in lover? Or maybe even a husband?' He raised dark brows.

'I believe I introduced myself as Eva Foster, the

same surname as Rachel's, and we've already established that she wasn't married when she died.'

'Not every woman changes her surname to that of her husband when she marries.'

He had a point, Eva conceded grudgingly. 'Not that it's any of your business, but no, I don't have a boyfriend, a live-in lover, or a husband I need to hurry back to,' she dismissed impatiently. 'I hadn't had the time for the latter before the twins were born, was too busy working, and then latterly caring for Rachel and the twins, and now I can't see any man being interested in taking on both me and my ready-made family!'

He nodded his satisfaction with her reply. 'Then there's no reason why you can't stay on in Paris for a week or two.'

'Stay on in Paris for a week or—!' Eva eyed him incredulously. 'There's one very good reason why I can't do that, Mr D'Angelo, and that reason is financial.' Honestly, did this man not live in the real world at all?

It had taken the last of Eva's savings to pay for the flight to Paris and the four nights' stay at the pension, and she simply couldn't afford to stay on any longer than that. It had all been a waste of her time and money anyway, which made the whole situation even worse!

'I wasn't for a moment suggesting—' Michael broke off what he had been about to say as a knock sounded on his office door. 'Come in,' he invited tersely, his scowl not lessening in the slightest as his dark-haired assistant manager opened the door to stand in the doorway. 'What is it, Pierre?' he demanded irritably as the other man looked at them both hesitantly.

Pierre grimaced his obvious discomfort at the interruption. *'Excusez-moi—'*

'You may as well stick with English, Pierre.' Michael tersely reminded the younger man that Eva Foster understood his French perfectly.

The younger man nodded. 'In that case, I thought I should remind you that you have a luncheon appointment with the Comte de Lyon at one o'clock, and it's twelve-thirty now,' he said in his perfect, unaccented English.

Michael gave an impatient glance at his wristwatch. 'So it is,' he realised impatiently. 'I'll need you to go to lunch with the Comte in my stead, Pierre,' he instructed briskly. 'Give him my apologies, and explain that—that an urgent family matter came up, which I had to deal with.'

Eva's cheeks burned with colour as she literally felt Pierre's curious brown gaze turning towards where she now stood near the floor-to-ceiling windows. When her own colouring and the twins' was so similar he would naturally jump to the conclusion, as most people did, that Eva was their mother.

Not that she thought for a moment that this elegant, handsome assistant of Archangel would press Michael D'Angelo on the subject; she doubted too many people ever dared to question this arrogantly decisive man on anything!

Besides which, Eva really wasn't interested in Michael D'Angelo's relationship with his staff, or his luncheon appointment with some French count. She was more concerned with finishing the conversation the two of them had been having before they were interrupted.

Was Michael D'Angelo seriously suggesting that she stay on in Paris for a week or two? What for? Whatever his reasoning he had better explain himself soon, because the twins would shortly be waking up and demanding their own lunch—probably at the top of their healthy lungs!

'And if the Comte is…unhappy with this arrangement?' Pierre prompted his employer.

'Then he'll just have to be unhappy,' Michael D'Angelo snapped. 'Just reschedule if that should be the case, Pierre,' he added dismissively as the younger man still looked uncertain.

A man, Eva realised, who had in all probability been working at Paris Archangel at the time Rachel was involved with Rafe D'Angelo…

'How long have you worked at Archangel, Pierre?' she prompted curiously, and instantly earned herself a frowning glance from Michael D'Angelo.

The younger man shot his employer a slightly startled glance before answering Eva's question. 'I—I have had the pleasure of being Assistant Manager here for almost four years now,' he answered her guardedly.

Eva gave a rueful smile at the man's tactful reply; she somehow doubted that was altogether true during the times when the forceful Michael was the D'Angelo brother in charge!

Her smile faded as she frowned. 'In which case, you will have been here—'

'We should let Pierre go to lunch now, Eva,' Michael interrupted her firmly, easily guessing where she was going with this conversation. And having Eva question the Archangel staff, or anyone else for that matter, as to whether or not they had known of her sister's relationship with Rafe fifteen months ago was exactly what Michael was trying to avoid happening.

'I'm sure Pierre doesn't mind my interest, Michael,' Eva returned the familiarity with saccharin sweetness. 'Especially when he finds it such a pleasure to work here.'

Michael eyed her sceptically, not fooled for a moment by that sweetness; Eva Foster had a tart little tongue in her beautiful head, one that he, and no doubt most of the men who met her, could easily imagine being put to better use. Eva Foster was seriously underestimating her own beauty and attraction if she believed having custody of the twins would deter most men from being attracted to her!

It was obvious, from the admiration gleaming in Pierre's gaze, that even a married man with two small children wasn't totally immune to the attraction of that glossy dark hair and those violet-coloured eyes!

'I'm afraid I have to insist,' Michael rasped harshly before turning to look at the younger man with narrowed eyes. 'I'm leaving now, Pierre, and won't be coming back to the gallery again today,' he informed the other man dismissively. 'So if you could see to the cancelling of my appointments for the rest of the day, and make sure that everywhere is locked up and ready for security before you leave this evening…?'

'Of course,' the younger man confirmed slightly dazedly. 'Mademoiselle,' he added politely to Eva Foster before leaving and closing the office door behind him, both men fully aware that hadn't been Michael's intention before Eva Foster had arrived at the gallery.

'You shouldn't have stopped me,' Eva Foster protested impatiently. 'He might have met Rachel, been able to confirm her relationship last year with your brother Rafe—'

'The only person I'm interested in confirming that relationship—or otherwise—is my brother Rafe,' Michael assured grimly.

'And he's unavailable!'

Michael scowled across at her. 'What do you want from me, Eva? Do you want me to interrupt Rafe's honeymoon and tell him about the twins—is that it?'

'Yes! No! I don't know...' she groaned unhappily.

'I can do that, if you demand it.' Michael nodded grimly; it was what most women would demand, so why should he expect this one to be any different? He didn't... 'No doubt it will irrevocably damage his marriage, but, yes, I can certainly contact Rafe right now if you insist upon it!'

'Stop trying to make me out to be the bad guy here!' Her eyes glittered with her own anger.

'Yes or no, Eva?' he pressed scathingly.

'I— No, of course I don't want to—to damage your brother's marriage before it's even begun, or hurt his wife, I just—'

'You've waited three months to come here looking for Rafe. Why can't it wait another couple of weeks?'

'Because it can't!'

'Why can't it?'

'Because—because—if you must know, because I'm almost broke! Okay?' she snapped defensively. 'The babies are very draining financially, and I haven't been able to work properly, and—and I'm broke!' she repeated emotionally.

Some of the tension left Michael's shoulders. 'And I'm suggesting you let me worry about that for the moment. If you wouldn't mind waiting here for a few minutes? I just have a few instructions I need to give to my secretary before we leave.' He strode over to the door.

'I— What do you mean, before "we" leave?' It had taken Eva several seconds to regroup, but now that she had…! It was one thing to agree that she wouldn't speak to Rafe D'Angelo until he came back from his honeymoon, quite another to accept any help from his arrogant brother. 'The only place I'm going is back to the *pension*, so that I can feed the twins and then call the airline to see if I can get our tickets changed to an earlier flight!'

'You're correct in assuming we're going back to your *pension*.' Michael D'Angelo nodded abruptly, his expression still grim.

Eva stilled as she eyed him warily across the

office. '*We* aren't going anywhere. At least, not together.'

'Oh, but we are, Eva,' he assured in a tone that brooked no argument.

Well…it might have brooked no argument from either Pierre or this man's secretary, but, as Eva wasn't one of Michael D'Angelo's employees, she had absolutely no intention of being browbeaten by this overpoweringly dominant man.

'No, we're not,' she answered him just as firmly before once again crossing the room to take charge of the handles of the double push-chair. 'If you wouldn't mind opening the door for me…?' She looked at him pointedly.

Michael frowned back at her with pure frustration. Did Eva really think that having come here and dropped this bombshell on him—on Rafe, and possibly the whole of his family—she was going to be allowed to just walk out again?

Perhaps she hoped that he would allow her to do just that, after Michael's threat earlier as to Rafe possibly wanting custody of the twins?

It certainly seemed that way…

And it was impossible for Michael not to admire her audacity as well as her stubbornness, as much as he had admired her beauty just minutes ago. Not too many people would dare to even attempt to thwart him, but Eva Foster obviously felt no hesitation in attempting to do just that!

As she had seemingly taken on the responsibility of her sister's two children without a thought for the impact it would have on her own life...?

It would seem so, he acknowledged begrudgingly.

Not only had it affected her ability to work at the career the warmth in her voice implied she loved—and which Michael had every intention of learning more about at the earliest opportunity, just as he intended learning much more about Eva Foster altogether—but she also believed it played a part in her inability to have a man in her own life.

Michael still thought she was seriously underestimating herself in that assumption, but nevertheless he also felt grateful that a man in her life was one less immediate complication he had to deal with.

And was that the only reason for him feeling an inner sense of satisfaction at knowing there was no man, either currently or in the recent past, in Eva Foster's life…?

Michael liked to keep his emotions guarded from the outside world, but that didn't mean he wasn't also completely honest with himself, and that honesty now demanded that he admit, inwardly at least, that he was deeply attracted to the fiery Eva Foster. And it was an attraction that annoyed him intensely.

And yet the attraction to her was there, nonetheless…

Possibly because at this moment he was clenching his hands into fists at his sides in order to stop himself from reaching out and touching the silkiness of her dark hair. And wanting to smooth those glossy black strands back from the pale perfection of her face as he gazed into those unusual violet-coloured eyes before he lowered his head to taste her soft and full lips with his own!

Also knowing that just a single taste wouldn't be enough, that he wanted to taste, to explore all of Eva Foster, from her glossy black head to her no doubt elegant toes.

Not only was this attraction particularly stupid on his part, in the current circumstances, because Eva Foster had openly admitted she wanted Rafe's financial help with the twins, but it also complicated the hell out of what Michael was planning to do next...

CHAPTER FOUR

'YOU CAN'T DO this!'

Michael sat in an armchair, elbows on the arms of that chair, fingers steepled together in front of him. He appeared totally relaxed and calm as he watched Eva pace restlessly up and down in the sitting room of his apartment, her eyes blazing like violet jewels, her cheeks flushed with temper. 'Forgive me for pointing this out…but, as the twins are already taking their afternoon nap in their cots in one of the bedrooms, it looks as if I already have done it.'

Eva faltered slightly before coming to a complete stop to glare across the room at him. 'And looking mighty pleased with yourself about it too!' she acknowledged disgustedly.

Michael shrugged his shoulders. 'I like it when my plans come together, yes.'

Eva looked as if she were about to explode at his latest 'plans'. 'You can't force me to stay here!'

Michael bit back his disappointment that the halt in her pacing had also put an end to his admiration of her curvaceous denim-clad bottom, something he had been enjoying immensely. 'I don't remember using any force?' He looked up at her between narrowed lids.

No, he hadn't, Eva acknowledged with frustration. Mainly because she hadn't realised what he was doing until it was too late, and she and the twins were already safely ensconced in the luxurious D'Angelo apartment, just a few minutes' walk down the Champs Élysées from the Archangel gallery!

Not that they had walked here immediately after leaving the gallery. Oh, no, first Michael had arranged for his car to drive them both to the *pension* where she and the twins were staying, and while she had been occupied feeding the twins their lunch he had been busy packing up the things she had taken out of the two suitcases when she arrived in Paris yesterday; she had packed as lightly as she could, but had still needed to bring two suitcases to carry all the paraphernalia necessary for travelling with two small babies.

By the time she had finished feeding the twins, and changed them both into clean clothes, Michael had been waiting at the door of her shabby room with those two suitcases already packed and sitting on the floor beside him.

Even then Eva hadn't realised exactly what his intentions were, had innocently imagined—as the sneer on his lips as he looked around the room had shown that neither it nor the pension came anywhere near this man's high expectations of accommodation—that he had decided to move them into a hotel until it was time for their flight back to England.

Never in her wildest dreams had Eva imagined that Michael intended moving her and the twins into the D'Angelo apartment. With him.

Or that one of those 'few instructions' he had needed to give his secretary before they had left the gallery was actually the buying of two cots, and the bedcovers to go with them, to be delivered immediately to his apartment for the twins to sleep in.

As for the D'Angelo apartment...!

Eva had been too nervous earlier, and then too agitated, to completely take in the elegance of

Michael's office at the Archangel gallery, only registering that it was luxuriously chic.

But this apartment—the D'Angelo family apartment, and used by all of them whenever they were in Paris, Michael had explained when they arrived here a short time ago—was the ultimate in elegant opulence.

It was also huge, taking up the whole of the top floor of this historic building, brown carpets on the floors, the walls papered with silk and pale cream throughout. There were original paintings and elegant mirrors adorning those walls, with gold filigree work to separate the panels down the hallway and in the sitting room, and crystal chandeliers hanging from every ceiling. Eva had no doubt that each and every piece of ornamentation or statuary was also a genuine antique.

The furniture in the sitting room was Georgian in design, an elegant chaise-longue in one of the bay windows looking down the Champs Élysées, with several other sofas and chairs covered in pale pink and cream striped silk, placed conveniently beside several delicate spindle-legged tables, each adorned with a unique and delicate ornament.

Eva's first thought, as she stood looking around that beautiful elegance, was that the twins, both able to crawl now, would demolish a beautiful room like this in just a few minutes. The brown carpet would be safe from their dribble and often food-besmeared fingers, but she didn't hold out the same hope regarding the silk-covered furniture and walls…!

Michael D'Angelo obviously had no appreciation of the destructive force of two six-month-old babies. And why should he? Eva very much doubted that he came into contact with babies at all in his day-to-day life. She hadn't appreciated the mess involved herself until she had sole custody of the twins. It hadn't taken her long to make her apartment in London babyproof: covers on the chairs, and everything moveable—knick-knacks, photographs, books et cetera—now put at a height Sophie and Sam couldn't reach.

All of those objections to the three of them staying here were without taking into account Eva's own, the primary one being she didn't want to stay here in this apartment with Michael D'Angelo!

He was too forceful, too unsettling, too disturbingly male, just too *everything* for Eva to even be able to think of sharing an apartment with him, even for the short time he demanded!

The bedroom Michael had informed her would be hers for the duration of her stay was beyond anything Eva could ever have imagined; the décor was all in gold and cream, delicate white furniture, gold covers and drapes on the white ornate four-poster bed, the carpets and curtains also gold, the painted ceiling an ornate display of cherubs and angels. It was the ultimate in luxury.

She gave a shake of her head. 'As soon as the twins wake up we're leaving.' She should never have allowed Michael to persuade her into putting them down for their afternoon nap in the first place. And she wouldn't have done if the twins, having eaten their lunch and ready for their nap, hadn't both been decidedly bad-tempered by the time they arrived at the D'Angelo apartment.

Michael arched dark brows. 'To go where, exactly?'

Eva's eyes narrowed. 'A hotel, or another *pension*, anywhere but here.'

'I thought you said you were low on funds?'

Her mouth thinned. 'You know, if I didn't al-

ready dislike you intensely, then your smug atti-
tude right now would certainly ensure that I did!'

Michael eyed her mockingly. 'Isn't it a little
early in our acquaintance for you to have decided
you dislike me as strongly as that?"

'Oh, I assure you, a little of your company goes
a long, long way!' she snapped. The less she had
to do with Michael D'Angelo in future, the better she would like it.

And not because she disliked him, intensely or
otherwise…

Eva hadn't shared an apartment with anyone
since her university days, and the thought of staying in this apartment now, night as well as day,
with a man as physically charismatic as Michael
D'Angelo, even with the twins as chaperones,
made her feel decidedly uncomfortable.

Not that Eva thought for one moment that Michael would ever return that physical attraction;
she just didn't think it was a good idea for her to
be alone with him here. If nothing else, she stood
a good chance of making a fool of herself if he
should ever realise her attraction to him!

Nor did she completely understand the reason

for him insisting that she and the twins stay here with him…

'I have absolutely no idea why you're smiling,' she bit out irritably, annoyed with herself as much as with Michael. For having noticed that he looked even more dangerously male when he smiled. Those black eyes became the colour of warm chocolate when he smiled instead of that cold black, and they were edged with laughter lines. Those same laughter lines beside curved and parted lips, showing very white and even teeth, and all revealing Michael D'Angelo for exactly what he was: a predatory male in his prime!

Michael didn't understand why he was smiling either. Laughter wasn't a predominant part of his nature at the best of times, and even more rarely when in the company of a beautiful woman. But Eva, with her apparent lack of a verbal filter, seemed to have found the ability to amuse him.

Even, it would seem, when she was telling him she disliked him intensely…

His humour faded as quickly as it had appeared. 'Neither do I,' he bit out coolly. 'But as you've agreed not to talk to Rafe until he returns from his honeymoon, I feel it best if you, and obviously the twins, stay here.'

'With you.'

'With me,' he confirmed evenly.

Warmth coloured her cheeks. 'That's hardly appropriate.'

Michael eyed her curiously, noting that telling colour in her cheeks, and the way her gaze refused to quite meet his. 'I wasn't suggesting that the two of us should share a bedroom, Eva, just the apartment,' he finally murmured slowly.

She looked even more flustered. 'I didn't think for a moment— It hadn't even occurred to me— You're being ridiculous!' she accused agitatedly.

The deepening blush in Eva's cheeks as he looked up at her was in complete contradiction to her claim of not having thought that for a moment…

'Am I?' Michael mused as he rose slowly to his feet, a hard smile of satisfaction curving his lips as he saw the way Eva instantly took a step back. Confirmation of her nervousness of being too close to him?

'Of course you are,' she snapped irritably.

'Why is that?' Michael knew that most women

wouldn't hesitate to take every advantage of their present situation.

Eva frowned her impatience. 'For one thing we don't even know each other—'

'And what we do know we dislike?' he suggested helpfully.

'I think the fact that you suspect me of being some sort of gold-digger, looking to fleece your brother out of his millions, and have treated me accordingly, speaks for itself!'

'You've openly admitted you want Rafe to give you money.'

'For the twins, not me!' she came back defensively.

If Michael was completely honest he was no longer so certain of Eva's motives, knowing it was his own past experience with Emma that had caused him to jump to that conclusion originally.

Admittedly he could see no similarity to Rafe in either of the twins, except perhaps the dark hair, but as Eva also had ebony-coloured hair it was logical to assume that her sister might have had similar colouring. But just because he didn't see any similarity to Rafe in the two babies didn't rule out the possibility of the twins being his brother's children. Eva seemed so certain that he was their father and there was no disputing the fact that Rafe *had* been in Paris fifteen months ago...

Michael grimaced. 'I'm willing to give you the benefit of the doubt on the subject. For the moment,' he added hardly.

'That's big of you!' she snapped sarcastically.

'I thought so,' he answered mildly.

'That's still no reason for you to deliberately embarrass me by making ridiculous remarks about the two of us sharing a bed!' She glared at him with those incredible violet-coloured eyes.

'And yet your blush would seem to imply you weren't entirely averse to the idea...?' he prompted hardly.

Eva looked nonplussed for a moment, and then that rebellious light came back into her eyes. 'Of course I blushed,' she bit out impatiently. 'The last thing I expected when I came to Paris was to...to be propositioned by Rafe D'Angelo's older brother!'

Michael shrugged. 'You would have found the idea less disturbing if I weren't Rafe's older brother?'

'I— You— But you are,' she finally managed to accuse impatiently. 'And, for the record, I find your warped sense of humour offensive.'

His mouth twisted derisively. 'You may not have known me very long, Eva, but I think you know me well enough to realise that I rarely, if ever, joke about anything...'

Yes, Eva did know that, had realised from the first that Michael D'Angelo was altogether too serious, which was the reason she'd had such difficulty imagining him and the fun-loving Rachel together. Correctly, as it happened.

But if Michael rarely, if ever, joked about anything did that mean that he was being serious now?

Of course he wasn't, she instantly chastised herself for her naiveté; Michael D'Angelo was just enjoying seeing her feel uncomfortable! And more fool her for allowing him to do so.

She snorted. 'If—and it's still a big if—I should decide to accept your offer and stay here with you until your brother gets back from his honeymoon, then you can be sure the two of us will be occupying separate bedrooms!'

'Let me know if you change your mind,' he drawled softly.

Eva looked at him searchingly, her stomach giving that lurching roll, palpitations in her chest, as though her heart was beating far too rapidly. She was unable to look away from the intensity of that jet-black and unblinking gaze. 'Why are you doing this?'

He raised dark brows. 'Maybe because I'm not averse to the idea of sharing a bed with you.'

Maybe, but he didn't look at all happy about it if that was the case, Eva realised slightly dazedly.

He grimaced on catching sight of her frown. 'Eva, I'm too old and cynical to play guessing games with a woman—'

'How old?' she put in quickly.

His mouth quirked into another smile, no doubt because of the incongruousness of her question; what did it matter how old Michael was, when Eva had no intention of becoming involved with him?

'Thirty-five,' he supplied softly. 'Too old for you?'

'I was just curious—' She broke off as she heard the sound of one of the twins crying out, quickly followed by another cry as the second baby was woken by the first.

'Babies *interruptus*...' Michael murmured mockingly. 'Let's put a "to be continued" sign on this conversation, hmm?'

'Let's not,' Eva dismissed firmly even as she turned and hurried from the sitting room to go to the twins.

Ran from the room better described it, Eva acknowledged ruefully as she gathered up both babies in her arms and quickly halted their crying.

Michael might have started out mocking her, but that conversation, the very air they both breathed, had seemed to become altogether too fraught with physical tension a few minutes ago.

With physical awareness...?

A physical awareness that would seem to imply Michael really might be attracted to her under all that cynicism...?

Despite the sudden intimate turn of their conversation, Eva had great difficulty believing that!

It wasn't just that Michael D'Angelo was such an aloofly arrogant and forceful man, there was also the fact that he so obviously didn't trust her, as well as the fact that he was way out of Eva's league, and she didn't just mean because of his immense wealth.

Ten years her senior, he was also a man of experience and sophistication, and, while Eva knew herself capable of being comfortable in any social setting, she certainly didn't play the sort of bed-hopping games so many other people enjoyed. People like Michael D'Angelo…

She wasn't a prude and nor was she a virgin, having been involved in one year-long relationship a couple of years ago, before the two of them had decided, quite amicably, that their two careers, hers in photography, his in accounting, made the relationship impossible to sustain; Eva had been away far too much on assignments, and they had eventually just drifted apart.

Eva hadn't been seriously involved with anyone since—hadn't so much as been out on a date since taking custody of the twins! She didn't think Michael D'Angelo, a man who so obviously had issues where trusting women was concerned, would be a good choice for her to think of taking the plunge with now either.

He might be as handsome as sin, but he was

also far too dominating, too intense in nature, too cold to be the sort of man Eva was attracted to. Most importantly of all, Michael was Rafe D'Angelo's brother!

And yet she was attracted to him, Eva acknowledged with a sinking heart. Maybe in part, because Michael was such a dominating, intense, and cold man…? There was a certain satisfaction in thinking that such a coolly self-contained man might find *her* attractive.

In wondering what sort of lover he would be…

Despite what she had thought earlier, would Michael lose that outer coldness when making love to a woman?

And how would it feel to have the freedom to touch and caress the hard planes of that lean and muscled body, to have Michael's long and elegant hands caressing her breasts, her thighs, and to have his lips and tongue explore and taste—?

'Everything okay?'

Eva spun round guiltily, her cheeks flushing a fiery red as she looked across at Michael standing in the bedroom doorway, at the fully clothed man who had just been at the centre of her erotic and very naked fantasy.

'Eva…?' He quirked a questioning brow as he obviously saw that guilty blush colouring her cheeks.

'Everything's fine,' she snapped irritably.

He continued to look at her searchingly between narrowed lids for several long seconds before nodding abruptly. 'I'm just going to change out of these formal clothes, and then we can decide what to do about our own lunch.'

Eva looked at him blankly. 'What to do about it…?'

'Whether to eat in or eat out,' he dismissed tersely. 'How much of Paris have you seen since you arrived?'

She grimaced. 'The inside of the *pension* and the scenery on the walk to your gallery this morning.'

Exactly what Michael had thought Eva would say. 'Then we'll eat out. If you would like to get together anything that the twins might need while I'm changing…?'

She gave a slow and wary shake of her head. 'I'm not expecting you to—to entertain me.'

'I thought we had agreed to put that particular conversation on hold…?' Michael gave a hard smile of satisfaction as he saw the becoming blush that instantly coloured those ivory cheeks.

'You know I didn't mean it in that way!' She shot him an irritated glare.

Of course Michael had known that. He just enjoyed seeing Eva blush. Just as he liked the idea that it was his teasing that had caused that blush.

Which was strange, because teasing, bantering word play wasn't something he usually bothered with where a woman was concerned. He had always preferred a more straightforward approach. Knowing that beneath a woman's desire there were always those pound signs.

And Eva Foster was no different in that regard, he reminded himself impatiently, the only difference being that it was Rafe she wanted money from.

His humour faded. 'I have no intention of entertaining you,' he bit out abruptly. 'We both need feeding, I don't cook, there's no housekeeper here, so the two of us going out to lunch is the logical answer.'

And Eva had a feeling that 'logic' was an important part of Michael's personality. That he preferred cool, calm practicality to any form of spontaneity. Quite where their previous conversation fitted into that cool logic she had no idea.

Although his mention of there being 'no housekeeper here' confirmed that, apart from the twins, the two of them really would be completely alone in his apartment...

'The four of us,' she corrected pointedly. 'And I think you might find that eating out with two small babies isn't as easy as it sounds,' she added ruefully.

That dark gaze flickered to the two currently quiet and contented babies Eva held in her arms. 'They seem happy enough at the moment.'

Eva smirked inwardly. He had no idea.

'I did try to warn you.' Eva gave the stony-faced Michael an amused glance between sooty lashes as they left the elegant restaurant situated along the embankment of the Seine, where he had decided they would stop and eat lunch.

It was a far less pristine Michael than the one who had left the apartment two hours ago, orange juice now visible down the front of his plain blue shirt, his casual black trousers damp from a glass of water Sam had knocked over, and slightly creased from where he'd had Sophie sitting on his knee for almost all of the meal.

If Michael had thought that Sophie and Sam would sit happily in their pushchair playing with their toes and gurgling happily while the two of them ate their meal, then he had been in for a rude awakening. The twins had fretted to be picked up within minutes of the two of them sitting down at the table, Eva knowing from experience that it was better for all concerned—namely the other people trying to eat their meals in peace—if she just picked them up rather than trying to reason with them. As Michael had tried to do initially. And very quickly learnt that six-month-old babies hadn't yet developed the capacity to be reasoned with.

It had been a very trying couple of hours.

Not least for Michael, who had obviously been totally at a loss as to how to amuse Sophie, let alone eat his food with one hand, which was all he'd had free when he was holding the baby in his other arm. It was a skill Eva had perfected in the past three months, always seeming to have one or other of the twins on her knee, sometimes both of them, whenever she tried to eat her meals.

'If you insist on us continuing to stay at your apartment, then perhaps we should shop for food and eat there in future…?' Eva suggested lightly as she wheeled the pushchair along the sun-dappled riverbank beside him, the majesty of the Eiffel Tower visible on the other side.

It was a view Eva would have loved to stop and photograph, if not for the fact that she had the broodingly silent Michael D'Angelo walking along beside her!

He shot her an irritated glance from beneath lowered dark brows. 'I am not about to let a six-month-old baby—or even two of them!—dictate where and when I eat my meals.'

'No?'

'No!'

Eva laughed softly at his determination. 'Even if it's easier?'

His mouth thinned. 'Easier doesn't make it acceptable.'

No, it didn't, and Eva could imagine that this man, so controlled, so serious, rarely took the easy way out in anything he did. Which was probably the main reason—surely the only reason—he had insisted that she and the twins stay at the apartment with him in the first place.

It was something Eva had been mulling over in her mind a lot during lunch.

Michael obviously wasn't convinced by her claim that his brother Rafe was the father of the twins. But he clearly had enough doubts that he was willing to accept this upheaval in his own life in order to keep them all exactly where he could see and hear them, until he was able to straighten things out once Rafe had returned from his honeymoon.

Because, she had realised, Michael had no intention of allowing her to repeat her claim about the twins' paternity to anyone else but him.

Oh, she had accepted that this couldn't have happened at a worse time for Rafe D'Angelo. She really wasn't a marriage wrecker, even if the marriage happened to be that of a man responsible for fathering the twins. She even understood Michael's reasons for deciding to keep her firmly under his watchful eye. But that didn't mean she had to like it.

Which was why Eva had felt a certain amount of amusement at Michael's obvious discomfort during lunch. He was inconveniencing her by insisting on detaining her in Paris; it seemed only fair that he should suffer a little of that same inconvenience himself.

And Eva knew from caring for the twins full time for the past three months that this was only the beginning of that inconvenience.

With any luck, Michael would be begging the three of them to leave Paris in just a few days' time...

CHAPTER FIVE

'IS IT LIKE this every night?'

'Like what…?' Eva turned from tidying up to look at Michael as he appeared in the doorway of the sitting room several hours later, pressing her lips together in an effort not to smile as she saw the disgusted look on his face as he eased the soaking wet front of his *third* clean shirt of the day away from his chest. 'Maybe you should go and change that,' she suggested, barely disguising a smirk.

'I intend to, but I'm seriously in need of a whisky first. Leave the tidying for now, and I'll help you do it later,' he advised as he walked over to the drinks cabinet. 'Like one?' He held up the decanter.

Why not? 'With lots of water, thanks,' she accepted lightly as she took his advice, and made herself comfortable on the sofa. 'Sophie appears to have taken a liking to you.' To the extent that her niece had squealed with pleasure when Michael had appeared in the bathroom doorway at bath time, Sophie smiling at him endearingly as she had held her arms up to him to be lifted out of the bath. A charm even the coolly self-contained Michael hadn't been immune to as he had then helped to put Sophie into her nightclothes before putting both babies down in their cots for the night.

'And you've been doing this on your own for three months?' He handed her the drink before sinking down gratefully into one of the armchairs.

Michael was surprised at how tired he felt; there was a lot more to this baby minding than he had ever realised.

For one thing, he had learnt that it was damned dangerous to take your eyes off crawling babies for even a few seconds, as Sam had proved when he had gone over to investigate the Venetian standard lamp and almost pulled it over on top of himself. And Sophie was into everything, constantly having to be distracted away from one disaster or another as she explored the room in detail.

Michael looked around that room now, too weary to even care that it was no longer the neat and tidy haven he had left this morning but now looked as if two mini tornadoes had swept through it.

'I really will finish tidying up in here in a minute,' Eva promised as she obviously saw his grimace.

'As I said, it will keep,' Michael dismissed. 'Is caring for babies always this…frenetic?'

She smiled ruefully. 'Today was a good day.'

Michael frowned as he recalled the chaos in the restaurant earlier today, the need to constantly pry little fingers away from danger since they had returned to the apartment, the coaxing necessary to get the twins to calm down enough to eat their tea, the splashing and squealing at bath time before the babies were placed clean and angelic-looking into their cots, both children having drifted off to sleep as Eva sang to them.

He gave a shake of his head. 'How have you managed on your own all these months?' This evening had been so chaotic he was seriously questioning his suspicions that Eva Foster was a gold-digger; surely no woman would willingly put herself through three months like the day he'd just spent with the twins if she didn't love them intensely!

She slipped off her shoes before tucking her legs up beneath her on the sofa. 'If you remember, I didn't have any choice in the matter.'

No, she hadn't, Michael acknowledged. With no parents, her sister also dead, and no help forthcoming from the father of the twins, there had only been Eva left to care for her niece and nephew. Michael was exhausted after spending only a few hours with them, and he hadn't been their main carer, just helping out occasionally when Eva obviously hadn't had enough hands to deal with them both at once.

How would Michael have coped in the same circumstances?

It was different for him, of course. He could afford to hire a nanny for the twins, two, if necessary. Eva, on the other hand, had not only lost her beloved sister three months ago, but she had also been left with the sole care of the twins, and obviously didn't have the money to pay for a single nanny to care for the babies, let alone two. Any more than she had enough money to pay for child-minders while she continued with her career. Whatever that career was…

And the strain of that had taken its toll, he realised as he looked across to where Eva now sat with her head leaning back against the sofa. Her eyes were closed, that ebony hair falling silkily onto the cream sofa cushions.

There were deep shadows beneath her closed lids, hollows in the paleness of her cheeks. Her face was all sharp angles, the skin stretched taut across high cheekbones, as if she had recently lost weight. Just as the clothes she had changed into after putting the babies to bed, a pale lemon T-shirt and black denims, seemed slightly loose on her slender frame.

If Eva really was a fortune-hunter then surely she would have sought out the twins' father— be it Rafe or some other man—much sooner than this? She certainly wouldn't have put herself through the hellish months of trying to cope with her sister's children on her own.

That was unfair. Eva hadn't just *tried* to cope; she had succeeded!

Until it had all become too much for her. Which

was when she had decided to seek out the help of the father of the twins…

A man she claimed was his brother Rafe.

Michael still had a problem believing that.

Because he didn't want to believe it, because of the complications it would cause in Rafe's life, in all their lives? Or because that was what Michael really believed?

Hell if he knew any more.

He did know that Eva believed it.

Just as he knew, by the way her whole body had now gone lax, the glass almost slipping from between her fingers, that Eva had fallen asleep!

Michael rose quickly to his feet to gently pluck the glass from her fingers before it fell to the carpeted floor and woke her up. He placed it gently down on the coffee table beside her before moving quietly about the room turning off most of the lamps, leaving only the Venetian lamp in the corner to cast a warm green glow over the room.

It was the perfect time for him to go to his bedroom and change out of his wet shirt—again—but he paused beside Eva for several seconds before doing so, frowning darkly as he looked down at her. She looked very young and vulnerable without that fierce pride glittering in those violet-coloured eyes and the defensive and angry flush to her cheeks, the stubborn set to her mouth, and the determined thrust to her pointed chin.

Eva had said this morning that she was in her mid-twenties. And already burdened down with two small babies that weren't even her own—although Michael now thought Eva might take exception to him using that phrase in reference to her custody of the twins she so obviously adored!

As she seemed to take exception to a lot of the things he had said to her today.

His previously well-ordered life was now in chaos, his workday totally destroyed, his apartment now invaded by three interlopers.

Because, until he had spoken to Rafe, Michael dared not do anything else but make sure this young woman stayed exactly where he could see her. No matter what the inconvenience or discomfort to himself.

And that was all without adding in the fact that Michael found himself unaccountably drawn to her, physically aroused by her, and in such a way that he knew having Eva's presence in his apartment for the next week or so, even with the twins as chaperones, was also going to play hell with his self-control...

She was light to his dark. Softness to his hardness. Warmth to his coldness. Laughter to his grimness.

In a word, Eva Foster was *dangerous*...

Eva woke slowly, momentarily disorientated as she stretched before opening her eyes to look about the unfamiliar and elegantly appointed room, taking several seconds to remember exactly where she was and why. And with whom.

Michael D'Angelo...

All six feet plus dark and broodingly disturbing inches of him!

Which posed the question, where was he?

Quickly followed by the realisation that she had fallen asleep without plugging in and turning on the vitally important baby monitor that would allow her to hear the twins cry out if they needed her.

Eva swung her legs quickly to the floor before sitting up abruptly, her head swimming slightly with the suddenness of the movement.

'Relax, Eva, the babies are both fine.'

She turned so suddenly towards the source of that voice she strained her already stiff neck, putting up a hand to soothe that stiffness as she frowned across to where Michael D'Angelo stood in the doorway. His hair looked dark, presumably from a recent shower, and a black T-shirt now stretched tautly over his muscled chest and flat abdomen, a pair of faded denims resting low down on his lean hips.

He looked...different, in informal clothes. More... Darker. Leaner. Sexier. So much more of the latter that Eva instantly felt the increased rate of her pulse as she continued to look at him, at the same time as she resisted the impulse to fold her arms to conceal the plumping arousal of her breasts.

'You shouldn't have let me sleep,' she accused defensively as a glance at her wristwatch showed it was almost nine o'clock.

'You were obviously tired...' Michael's eyes had narrowed, not at the aggressiveness of her tone, but because he was wondering what had caused the becoming flush that now coloured Eva's previously pale cheeks, her eyes a dark and unfathomable violet between sooty lashes. 'Dinner should be delivered in a few minutes,' he added distractedly.

She pushed back the dark swathe of her hair, revealing the delicate network of veins at her brow. 'Pizza?'

He smiled slightly. 'A four-course meal and the appropriate wines from André's.'

She raised dark brows as she obviously recognised the name of one of the most exclusive restaurants in Paris. 'Normal people just order pizza…'

'I would hope I'm a normal person, Eva. I just also happen to like good food.' Michael gave an unapologetic shrug. 'I also thought we both deserved more than a snack for dinner as our lunch was such a disaster.'

'Oh, I'm not complaining,' she assured ruefully. 'And I hate to tell you this, but lunch was a typical example of mealtimes with the twins!'

Michael had already guessed that, which was another reason he had decided to order the meal from André's; Eva's slenderness was a clear indication that she was in need of an uninterrupted meal, cooked by someone else.

Although Michael wasn't quite so sure, with

his increasing physical awareness of her, about
the two of them eating dinner alone together in
the intimacy of the adjoining dining room… 'I
thought we could eat in the kitchen?' he prompted
briskly.

'Fine with me.' Eva nodded as she stood up
to stretch her cramped limbs. 'I can't remember
the last time I slept so deeply…' she added with
a frown.

He shrugged broad and unconcerned shoulders.
'You obviously needed it.'

Yes, she had. She had been with her sister constantly during the last seven months of Rachel's
life, and the past three months had been spent
sleeping with half an ear open in case one or both
of the twins needed her.

Eva had no doubt that she owed the deepness
of the nap she had just taken to the fact that she
had known instinctively that she could trust Michael D'Angelo to deal with any emergency that
might occur while she was sleeping.

He exuded an assured self-confidence that
seemed innate, Eva acknowledged as she now
looked at him beneath lowered dark lashes. An
air of competence as well as confidence.

Just as he also exuded an inherent sexual aura that Eva knew would prevent her from ever feeling completely relaxed in his company…

It was the fact that Michael seemed so unaware, or more likely just uninterested, in the impact of his own sexual attraction on women that made that attraction all the more lethal.

In fact, Eva could never remember being so totally physically aware of a man as she was of the enigmatic Michael D'Angelo at this moment.

Maybe it was because his hair was still damply tousled from the shower, and the informality of the fitted T-shirt and denims made him appear far removed from the cold and incisive businessman she had met at the gallery earlier this morning.

Either way, this awareness, this pulse-pounding body-heating attraction she now felt towards Michael, was totally inappropriate in the circumstances!

'I think—'

'I'll just—'

Eva's cheeks flushed slightly as she looked across at Michael questioningly.

'I'll just go and put out the cutlery and glasses in the kitchen,' he finished dryly.

Eva nodded. 'And I'll go and check on the twins and then finish tidying up in here.' It wouldn't take her more than a few minutes; the wreckage the twins left in their wake always looked worse than it was.

Michael grimaced. 'I would have done it, but I didn't want to wake you.'

She smiled. 'Thanks.'

Michael continued to look at Eva for several long seconds as he found himself slightly transfixed by the brightness of her smile; her eyes now glowed a warm violet, her cheeks were rosily flushed, the lushness of her lips relaxed and slightly parted to reveal straight and even teeth.

Eva Foster, when she wasn't looking angry or harassed, was indeed a very beautiful woman.

Damn it, she was still beautiful even when she was looking angry or harassed!

And this was only day one of his self-imposed nightmare…

Day one became day two, and then day three, and with each successive day Michael's awareness of Eva Foster deepened to the point he had felt himself more than once balanced on the edge of taking her in his arms and kissing her. He had nothing but admiration for the selfless way in which she had devoted herself to caring for her sister's twin babies.

Michael spent his days at the gallery, but Eva and the twins were there waiting for him in his apartment when he returned each evening, and the two of them had fallen into the routine of feeding and bathing the twins together before Michael ordered dinner to be delivered from one of the exclusive restaurants he usually frequented but was currently unable to do so.

They talked as they ate those meals together, exchanging views on everything and nothing. But, as if by tacit consent, neither of them talked of Rafe, or what would happen when his brother returned from his honeymoon.

It was…domesticated. Pleasantly so, in fact, when Michael had always believed that domesticity wasn't for him.

As for Eva…

Each minute, each hour, Michael spent in her company only served to deepen his attraction to her, to increase his physical awareness of her, to a degree that he had begun to take cold showers before going to bed in an effort to resist the ever-increasing desire he felt to walk the short distance down the hallway that separated their two bedrooms!

By the third evening of Eva's stay Michael knew his normally rigid control was seriously shaken, so much so he was no longer sure a cold shower was going to be anywhere near enough of a deterrent for the increasing ache he felt to make love with her...

'That was another delicious meal.' Eva gave Michael a smile of satiation as he sat across the kitchen table from her watching her intently as she finished the last of the lemon mousse he had ordered for their dessert; Michael certainly knew some amazing Parisian restaurants to order food from!

To her surprise the past two days had been more relaxed than she could ever have hoped for in the circumstances, her days spent sightseeing with the twins, her evenings enjoying eating a leisurely and always delicious meal with Michael.

And, Eva realised, she had enjoyed Michael's

company as much as, if not more than, the delicious food!

He had proved to be both an intelligent and provocative dining companion as they discussed but respected their often differing views on everything from education to global warming. And art. They discussed art, in all its forms, a lot. Which Eva especially loved; it had been too long since she had been able to sit down with another adult and enjoy any intelligent conversation, let alone about her favourite subjects.

And if all of that conversation and those amazing and companionable meals had succeeded in heightening Eva's awareness of this relaxed and informal Michael D'Angelo, then that was her problem to deal with, because, her own reservations aside, she knew she was the last person Michael would ever *allow* himself to be attracted to.

He looked across at her quizzically now. 'You still haven't explained how it is you've travelled so extensively...?'

Her smile became wistful. 'It was part of my job. I used to be a photographer,' she explained at Michael's questioning look.

'Well...I suppose I'm still a photographer. Of

sorts,' she added with a grimace. 'Only I've taken a step backwards, and now just do the occasional wedding and christening!'

Michael gave a slow shake of his head. 'And what did you used to photograph?'

'Oh, this and that.' Eva shrugged dismissively, reluctant to talk about what she used to do.

Because it was too painful.

Much as she loved the twins, and was more than happy to stop travelling on assignments while they were so young and needed her with them, she still couldn't help but feel a pang of longing for the career she had necessarily put on hold. It wasn't for ever, Eva consoled herself—the twins would grow up, go to school, and then maybe she could think about resuming at least part of her career.

In the meantime having the twins meant she still had part of her sister with her. That she could enjoy watching the twins grow up, and telling them, when they were old enough, of the mother who had loved them. Loved them so much she had been willing to die to give them life…

Michael eyed her searchingly as he noticed the sudden sheen of tears in those violet-coloured eyes. 'Why the reluctance to talk about your work, Eva?'

She shrugged. 'I just don't see the point in talking about the past, that's all.'

No, that wasn't all, Michael recognised shrewdly. Whatever Eva's photographic career had been, her reluctance to talk about it now would seem to indicate it was something she had loved doing.

Something she'd had to give up in order to care first for her sister, and then the twins.

Which forced Michael to acknowledge that he hadn't carried out his initial decision: to find out everything he could about Eva Foster...

Not surprising when his days had been spent so busily at the gallery and his evenings just as busy with Eva and the twins!

Or maybe, inwardly, he had been harbouring the hope that Eva would be the one to tell him about herself...?

'And if I'm interested...?' he prompted softly.

'That's just too bad,' she dismissed impatiently as she stood to begin collecting up the last of the dishes from their meal before carrying them over to the counter.

Michael turned in his chair so that he could continue looking at her, watching the suppleness of her body as she loaded the dishwasher, even as he tried to puzzle out this woman who had somehow managed to fascinate him, in spite of himself.

These past few days had been unlike any others he had ever known, and not just because the twins had burst into his life. No, the main reason was Eva, and his interest in her, his attraction to her in spite of himself, and his enjoyment in her company.

He loved his family, enjoyed his work at the galleries, but the women who came briefly into and then out of his life never even came close to knowing the real Michael. Probably because he chose those women for their physical and social attributes, and they chose to be with him, however briefly, because he was one of the wealthy and influential D'Angelo brothers.

At a little over five feet tall, with a lean, slender figure—apart from those firm and thrusting breasts!—Eva Foster was nothing at all like the sophisticated spa-and-beauty-parlour-enhanced women he briefly dated.

Just as Eva had made it clear from the beginning that she didn't consider his being one of the wealthy and influential D'Angelo brothers as being an asset as far as she was concerned!

As a result, these past few days had been the first time, ever, that Michael had felt as if he and a beautiful and desirable woman had talked openly, honestly, to each other.

And he didn't want that to change by having Eva clam up on him now.

'Perhaps if you— Wait a minute!' Michael sat forward alertly as an idea suddenly occurred to him. An idea that maybe should have occurred to him much sooner than this! 'Eva Foster...' he murmured slowly, sharply. 'Is it possible that you're the photographer E J Foster?' He looked across at her searchingly.

Eva blinked as she straightened from loading the dishwasher, her shoulders tensed defensively. 'How do you know about E J Foster?' she prompted as she looked across at him warily.

'I co-own and run three art galleries, Eva,' Michael reminded dryly. 'And I consider E J Foster's photographs to be art in its purest form!'

'You do…?' A delicate—and pleased?—flush now coloured her cheeks. As evidence that she was indeed E J Foster?

'I do.'

Eva couldn't help but feel a certain amount of pleasure in Michael's praise of her work. After all, no matter what her personal gripe was against the D'Angelo family, he *was* Michael D'Angelo, one of the three brothers who owned the prestigious Archangel galleries, and a man, an expert, whom she knew the art world held in deep respect.

Michael stood up abruptly. 'Come with me.' He held out his hand to her.

Eva's wariness increased, her expression guarded as she still held back. 'Come where?'

'With me,' Michael pressed decisively as he continued to hold out his hand invitingly.

Eva wasn't at all sure about this. Admittedly the two of them seemed to have reached an uneasy truce, considering that Michael suspected her of trying to coerce money out of his brother, and the fact that she wasn't at all happy about his suggestion that his brother Rafe might perhaps want a hands-on role in his children's lives.

But Michael was certainly acting very strangely now…

Nor did she feel in the least reassured when she reluctantly took his hand—a strong and firm hand that swallowed up her much smaller one as he curled his fingers about hers—and he led her out of the kitchen and down the hallway in the direction of the bedrooms.

His own bedroom, Eva realised as he opened a door at the end of the corridor and flicked on a light switch, illuminating two paintings on the opposite wall, but otherwise leaving the room in darkness.

Even so Eva could see that the décor was in browns and creams, the carpet a dark chocolate-brown, the drapes at the windows of cream brocade, the four-poster bed a dark and masculine mahogany and draped with the same cream brocade.

But the added giveaway to this being Michael D'Angelo's own bedroom was the suit he had been wearing earlier draped over the mahogany chair in front of the masculine dressing table, a pair of highly polished black leather shoes tucked neatly beneath that chair, and a set of gold cuff-links glittering on the dressing-table top.

Eva instinctively pulled back from entering his obviously personal domain, although she didn't succeed in freeing her fingers from his. 'I don't know what you have in mind, but I think I should warn you that I'm really not— What are you doing?' she protested as Michael released her hand, only to take a firm hold of her arms and push her further into the bedroom. 'Michael...?'

'There!' Michael stood behind her, keeping that light grasp on both her arms as he faced her towards one of the paintings illuminated on the bedroom wall.

Except it wasn't a painting.

There, on Michael D'Angelo's bedroom wall, was a large, framed, limited edition photograph. A photograph Eva easily recognised. Because she had taken it...

CHAPTER SIX

IN THE FOREGROUND of the photograph was a young African woman, her baby strapped to her back with a wide strip of coloured material, and above and behind her, silhouetted in the setting sun, was a lioness lying on the flat rock of an escarpment, her cub at her feet. A small gold plaque on the base titled it 'Harmony'.

Eva blinked back the tears as the photograph brought back memories of that last evening of her stay in Africa. She had spent over a week at the tribe's encampment, listening to their stories, and had taken dozens of photographs. But this particular photograph, of the woman and her baby, the lioness and her cub atop that escarpment, she had taken on her last evening there, and it held special meaning for her.

It represented the harmony of man and nature, living together, each respecting the other's right to be there. Even if that occasionally led to one or other of them being killed…

'There's something more to the photograph, isn't there?' Michael prompted gruffly, intensely, the photograph affecting him emotionally, as it usually did.

Eva looked at him sharply. 'How did you know that?'

He shrugged broad shoulders. 'I just did.'

Moisture dampened her eyes as she nodded before turning back to the photograph. 'The mother had lost her older child when this same lioness attacked the village a few weeks earlier.' She spoke in a hushed voice, as Michael had, as if they might disturb the mother or the lioness if they spoke too loudly. 'The men of the village tracked the lioness down, left her unharmed, but killed one of her two cubs.

'They saw it as balance, that with only one cub to feed the lioness would not be hungry enough to attack their village a second time.' She gave a shake of her head. 'I talked to the mother for hours, and, while she deeply mourned her lost child, she harboured no ill will towards the lioness for wanting to nurture her own children, and, as you can see, she felt no fear either. She just accepted the balance, the—the—'

'Harmony,' Michael murmured softly, appreciatively.

Eva swallowed. 'Yes. I don't think I could be as…understanding of that balance or harmony, if it had been one of the twins who had been taken.'

'No,' he accepted huskily, understanding that Eva's perspective would certainly have changed with the advent of the twins into her own life. 'But even so, at the time you understood, totally encapsulated this mother's acceptance of that balance and harmony, in your photograph.'

Eva breathed softly. 'I— How did you get this?'

'The same way every other lucky person at the E J Foster exhibition in London eighteen months ago acquired their own exclusive photograph—I bought it,' Michael stated with satisfaction, remembering how he had been drawn to this image that evening. He had been determined, compelled, to own it.

He'd had no idea he would one day meet the photographer under such unusual circumstances.

'You weren't at the gallery that evening…?' If she had been Michael would have made a point of being introduced to her. And, in view of his attraction to her now, it was anyone's guess where that introduction might have led...

She drew in a sharp breath. 'No. I— It was the night of my parents' car accident.' She gave a shake of her head. 'They were on their way to the exhibition when another car went through a red light and hit them head-on. They were both killed instantly. The exhibition didn't seem important after that.'

'God, I'm sorry...' Fate, it seemed, had found a cruel way to intercede in the two of them not meeting before now.

'That was the first, and last, exhibition of my work,' Eva acknowledged wistfully.

'Why?'

She smiled ruefully as she shrugged. 'Life— and obviously death—got in the way.'

Michael nodded. 'Your parents, then the twins and your sister.'

'Yes.'

'You said you were out of the country when Rachel discovered she was pregnant...?'

'Tibet,' Eva confirmed.

'Photographing for another exhibition?'

'Yes,' she sighed.

'An exhibition that never happened.'

'No.' Eva still had the photographs on her camera, but hadn't had the time, or the inclination, to do anything with them since returning to England.

And she now found it weird, too uncomfortably strange, that Michael D'Angelo, of all people, should have one of her earlier photographs displayed on his bedroom wall. She couldn't even attempt to dismiss or make light of it.

Stranger still that Michael had sensed, known, there was more to the photograph than could be seen with the naked eye...

It was an intuition, a sensitivity, she would never have expected from the coldly brisk businessman she had met at Archangel that first morning, in his expensive tailored suit, silk shirt and soft Italian leather shoes.

The same man who had initially treated her with such suspicion, and who still didn't trust her not to bring shock waves of scandal to his family, simply because she could. To the point that Michael had preferred to invite her and the twins to invade his own personal space, namely this Parisian apartment, rather than allow her to return to England before he'd had the opportunity to confirm or deny her claim by speaking to his brother Rafe.

That man, that coldly aloof and arrogantly forceful man, had exhibited none of the inner sensitivity Michael had revealed to her these past two days, and had just reinforced, by his complete understanding of one of her African photographs...

Because, as Eva had come to realise, Michael D'Angelo was a man of many layers. Layers she now suspected he had deliberately put in place in order to guard himself and his emotions. She had no idea what—or possibly who—had caused this reaction in him, only knew that they were layers he allowed very few, if any, to peel away to reveal the sensitive man hidden beneath.

No doubt his family knew the real Michael.

And the twins, in their innocence, had recognised, had known instinctively from the beginning, the emotionally sensitive man that lay beneath that outer veneer of cold urbanity, and they had been drawn to him, had trusted him.

Eva would have preferred, it would have been

safer, if she had never so much as glimpsed that man beneath those layers…

Because she was far too aware of Michael already. Against her will—her loyalty to her sister—she had found him overpoweringly attractive as the co-owner of the Archangel galleries, dressed in his dark and exquisitely tailored business suits. But she found him even more so in the casual T-shirts and faded denims he changed into in the evenings, both emphasising the lean strength of his body, while at the same time doing nothing to diminish the leashed sensuality of the man wearing those clothes.

'I had always assumed E J Foster was a man.'

Eva turned to him in surprise. 'Why?'

'I have no idea,' he acknowledged gruffly, eyes glittering darkly as he continued to look up at the photograph rather than at Eva. 'I really should have known… It's so obvious to me now that a woman took this photograph,' he added ruefully. 'It's there, in the gentle way the fading light picks up the darkness of the baby's eyes as its head rests tiredly against its mother's shoulder, in the smooth turn of the mother's cheek as she gazes up at the lioness with its own cub. I believe a man would have concentrated on the majesty of the lioness and cub, rather than the more gentle beauty and calm of the mother and her baby.'

Eva felt slightly...unnerved—*very* unnerved!— by this further example of Michael's insight into what her feelings had been that evening in Africa, because those had been exactly her emotions as she photographed the woman and lioness. And Michael had known that just from looking at the photograph. So much so that he had wanted to own it...

Her discomfort, her awareness of him, in this dimly lit bedroom, increased exponentially.

It was so quiet in this part of the apartment, no sound of traffic or people, just the soft sound of their joint breathing, and the dim lighting to add to the air of intimacy.

An intimacy Eva knew she desperately needed to break—before she did something incredibly stupid!

In fact, now would definitely be a good time for one of the twins to cry out for attention!

No such luck, she realised, as the rest of the apartment outside this bedroom remained completely, eerily, silent...

Eva moved abruptly to look at the second illuminated frame, frowning as she found herself looking up at a painting of a single red rose. A dying rose, the blood-red petals falling softly down onto the base of the canvas. 'This painting is…' She broke off, lost for words as to both the poignant beauty and starkness of the subject of the painting.

'Allegorical,' Michael provided huskily.

'Yes.' Eva nodded, having known immediately that the painting represented so much more than the dying of that beautiful, perfect rose.

Just as she knew that the death of the rose would represent different things to different people. In some, the death of hopes. In others, dreams. And to many, love…

The question was, which of those things did it represent to Michael, a man Eva hadn't initially believed to be capable of any of those softer feelings, but had come to see differently?

He was a wealthy and successful businessman, so she very much doubted that he had any unfulfilled hopes and dreams in the professional side of his life.

Which left his personal life, and the possible

death of love. Or perhaps trust...? Which would go a long way to explain his distrust of her initially, a distrust she had realised was slowly fading...

Michael was still single. And completely unattached romantically? Eva had never thought to ask! Had he once hoped for more? Had he loved and lost, a loss this painting represented to him?

Eva couldn't imagine any woman wanting to walk away from the intensity of emotions she was now so sure Michael was capable of feeling.

So perhaps it wasn't the painting itself, but the artist, that meant something to him?

'Bryn Jones.' She read the name of that artist in the bottom right corner of the painting. 'I saw pictures of some of the pieces from her exhibition online. She's an amazing new artist, isn't she?' And perhaps meant more than that to Michael?

'And my sister-in-law,' he provided huskily. 'Bryn is now married to my youngest brother Gabriel,' he added as Eva looked at him curiously.

'Oh.' Eva frowned as that theory crashed and burned. 'It's...a beautiful painting.'

Michael chuckled. 'But sad,' he acknowledged wryly. 'So very sad...'

'Yes.' What else could she say? It *was* a sad painting. Very much so. And a reflection of Michael's own inner emotions? Of his disillusionment, with life or love? Or possibly both?

Eva would much rather not think of Michael in that way. Much preferred to keep him at arm's length, emotionally as well as physically, rather than finding herself, as she now believed she did, understanding the emotional man that lay beneath that outer veneer of cold severity.

A veneer that Eva found she saw less and less the more time she spent in Michael's company...

'Bryn tells me she's painting its opposite—a red rose in full bloom—for her next exhibition,' he revealed.

Eva arched dark brows. 'In the hopes you'll buy it?'

'Apparently not.' He gave a rueful shake of his head. 'The painting will make an appearance at the exhibition, but it won't be for sale; Bryn insists on giving it to me as a gift. In the hope, she says, that it will help me to eventually see and feel love the way she and Gabriel do.' He grimaced. 'It's a little sickening to hear someone as lovely as Bryn talking about my little brother in those terms!'

And Michael, Eva realised shrewdly, with that last remark, was deliberately deflecting the conversation away from what his first comment had revealed...

Michael *had* once loved and lost, Eva acknowledged uncomfortably. It might have been many years ago, rather than recently, but Eva had no doubt that an artist of Bryn Jones' calibre would also have been able to see, as she now did, the man beneath that outer shell of cold aloofness. A veneer he had chosen to adopt because of that lost love?

It was significant, Eva thought, that Michael kept the painting in the privacy of his bedroom rather than on public view in any of the main rooms of the apartment.

As he did her African photograph...

Eva felt another quiver of awareness down the length of her spine, an increase in the tension in the air, at the intimacy of knowing Michael kept one of her photographs on the wall of his bedroom. She had always felt that all of her photographs were a part, an extension, of herself. And it was a little unnerving to know that all this time Michael would have looked at this particular photograph on a daily—and nightly—basis!

Of course he wouldn't, she instantly chastised herself. Not only was Michael a businessman, which meant he no doubt considered both the painting and the photograph as investments, but he had told her himself that he and his two brothers rotated the management of the three Archangel galleries, here, New York and in London. Which meant that Michael would only be in Paris for a maximum of four months a year—

'The painting and the photograph travel on the D'Angelo plane with me wherever I live,' he said huskily.

Eva frowned her impatience as she turned. 'Why did you tell me that?' she snapped irritably.

Because Michael had been able to see, to know, the thoughts that had been running around in Eva's beautiful head just now. Because all of Eva's thoughts, and her emotions, were becoming easier for him to read.

And a few minutes ago she had definitely been in the process of putting both Bryn's painting, and her own photograph, in a neat little box, no doubt marked 'Michael D'Angelo's investments'!

Oh, there was no doubting that the painting and photograph could both be classed as investments; they just meant so much more to him than that, to a degree that Michael knew he would never sell either one of them.

To have now realised, to know, that Eva was E J Foster, the photographer of 'Harmony', was… unsettling, to say the least.

Michael had attended the exhibition of E J Foster's photographs that night eighteen months ago without too much hope of finding anything to interest him. His acceptance of the invitation had been more of a courtesy to a fellow gallery-owner than anything else. Photography wasn't a medium that had ever particularly meant anything to Michael. It had certainly never touched him emotionally, the way a painting or sculpture could.

He had been impressed by the E J Foster photographs at first glance, and totally hooked the moment his eye had caught 'Harmony'. Had felt himself being drawn into the photograph, along with an instant affinity with the raw emotion and majesty of the subject.

And the photographer?

Perhaps.

But until this evening Michael had assumed that E J Foster was a man, allowing his own emotions to be centred on the photograph rather than the photographer. To now know that Eva was that 'man', and the history behind the photograph, a history he had only been able to guess at before this evening, somehow now seemed to give Michael that same affinity with her...

'Michael...?'

He looked at Eva through narrowed lids, his breath catching in his throat, his pulse pounding loudly, as he saw how beautiful she looked in the dimmed lighting of his bedroom, her eyes a deep and drowning purple.

It had been a serious mistake to bring her to his bedroom at all, Michael now realised as another part of his anatomy began to pulse and harden to the heated rhythm of the blood that now pounded through his veins as he found himself captured, ensnared, by those deep purple wells of emotion.

Deep purple wells of desire?

The same desire that now held Michael in its thrall?

Eva could almost feel, touch, the intensifying, the thickening of the air as it now seemed to still about them, as she and Michael continued to stare at each other in the semi-darkness of his bedroom, only the light spilling in from the hall-way and over the two picture frames to illumi-nate the room.

Eva barely felt able to breathe, certainly couldn't look away, or move so much as a finger in protest, as Michael's gaze continued to hold hers and his head slowly began to lower towards hers.

Her heart leapt in her chest, electricity now charging the air about them as she felt the first, exploratory, questioning touch of those chiselled lips against her own, before they hardened, tak-ing control, as Michael obviously felt her re-sponse.

Eva's hands moved up to grasp onto the broad-ness of Michael's shoulders as her knees went suddenly weak, instantly feeling the heat of the hard flesh beneath her fingers, and the muscled strength of Michael's chest as his arms moved about her waist and he pulled her in closer against him.

She groaned low in her throat even as her lips parted to the moist and rasping brush of Michael's tongue, that marauding tongue instantly seeking, exploring, the heat of her mouth as he held her even closer, making Eva fully aware of the throbbing heat and fullness of his arousal as it pulsed long and thick against her abdomen.

It was a desire Eva knew she felt too as her breasts swelled with arousal, the nipples becoming hard and aching berries as that heat now swelled, dampened, between her thighs, her whole body on fire with need as she returned the intensity of Michael's kisses.

Heated kisses that deepened, grew hungrier still, as Eva felt the warmth of Michael's hand against the bare flesh of her abdomen beneath her T-shirt, moving slowly and caressingly upwards, until that hand cupped the fullness of her breast, the soft pad of Michael's thumb a soft caress against the aching tip.

Eva wrenched her mouth from Michael's in a gasp, her throat arching as the heat of his mouth trailed across her cheek to the sensitive column of her throat, and then lower still as he pushed up the barrier of her T-shirt before taking the fullness of her nipple into the heat of his mouth, suckling deeply even as his tongue moved in a rough and sensuous rasp across the plump nipple.

Eva's knees threatened to buckle as desire coursed through her body in hot, pulsing waves, her fingers becoming entangled in the dark thickness of his hair as between her thighs swelled, ached, moistened in invitation, Eva needing, wanting more.

And Michael gave her more as he transferred the attention of his mouth and tongue to her other breast, the v between her thighs becoming an urgent needing throb as his hand moved down to cup her there.

'I need—oh, God, I need—Michael…?'

'Do you trust me to know, to give you what you need, Eva?' Michael groaned urgently.

'Yes…! Just— Please!' She was going out of her mind with desire, with aching need, had to have relief from the pleasure that now surged and swelled inside her in hot and consuming waves.

Michael's lips and tongue returned to caressing and suckling her sensitive breast as he curled one arm about her shoulders, the other beneath her knees, before he lifted her up into his arms and carried her over to the bed, placing her gently down on top of it before joining her there.

He moved up on his knees between her parted thighs as he pulled her T-shirt up and over her head before throwing it to one side as he then feasted his eyes on the bareness of her breasts. Full and swollen mounds that fitted perfectly into the palms of his hands as he cupped them, and tipped by deep rose-coloured and engorged nipples.

Michael's gaze held Eva's as he slowly lowered his head to suckle first one nipple and then the other, knowing he had never tasted anything so exquisite; her skin was so soft, and tasted of warmed honey.

It was a taste he could all too easily become addicted to!

He continued to hold Eva's gaze as he kissed down the leanness of her abdomen, her eyes dark and glittering between sooty lashes, her cheeks flushed, her lips red and moistly swollen from their earlier kisses.

Would those lips between her thighs be as swollen, as red, as glistening with that same arousal? Would they have the same honey taste?

Michael ached to know!

Had to know.

To *taste*…

Michael looked down at her between narrowed lids as he sat up on his knees once again before releasing the button on Eva's denims and slowly sliding the zip downwards, allowing her the opportunity to stop him if she wanted to; he had never forced himself on a woman in his life, and he wasn't about to start now. No matter how much he might want, *ache*, to taste Eva.

Thankfully, she made no move to stop him, not when he shifted to one side to take off her shoes before peeling her jeans down her thighs and removing them completely, nor when he hooked his fingers into her tiny black silk panties and they met the same fate. Instead she closed her eyes completely, her hands falling to the bedcovers beside her as Michael once again knelt between her legs, allowing him to look his fill between her parted thighs.

Her curls here were as ebony as the hair on her head. Silky soft and slightly damp curls that revealed her mound and the glistening and swollen lips beneath.

'Beautiful...' he groaned huskily as he parted her legs even wider before slowly moving to lie between her thighs and lowering his head.

Eva groaned just at the feel of the warm heat of Michael's breath against her sensitivity, that groan turning to a soft keening, her hands moving up instinctively to become entangled in the dark thickness of his hair at the first hot sweep of his moist tongue.

She lost all sense of where she was, who she was, as that plundering tongue continued to lathe hot and rhythmically, endlessly, hard and then soft, circling and then pressing, and almost, but not quite, taking her over the edge into the maelstrom of release.

'No...!' she groaned in protest as Michael raised his head, only to groan anew as he moved lower and she felt his fingers moving to caress, to stroke her most sensitive spot, as the moist length of his tongue probed, and then pierced through the throbbing lips at the entrance to her sheath, before plunging hotly, deeply inside. Taking her, possessing her as his other hand moved up to her breast, capturing, caressing, gently squeezing the fullness of her nipple between finger and thumb in the same rhythm as his thrusting tongue and stroking fingers.

Eva's hips arched up off the bed as she once again felt the hot sweep of Michael's tongue against her pulsing core, even as his fingers parted her swollen folds before thrusting inside, first one, and then two, stretching those quivering muscles, fingers curling slightly as he sought, and found that place deep inside her to stroke with each thrust of his fingers.

Eva's hips continued to arch up, again and again, as she met each and every one of those thrusts, until she cried out, sobbed, her fingers tightly clasping the coverlet as the fierceness of her orgasm surged through her whole body in hot and burning release, threatening to tear her apart with its ferocity. Tears burned down Eva's cheeks as wave after never-ending wave of pleasure took her beyond anything she had ever known before.

As *Michael* took her beyond any other pleasure she had ever known before…

CHAPTER SEVEN

'Did I hurt you?' Michael frowned his concern as he moved up the bed to lie beside Eva, fingers gentle as he touched the tear-wet cheeks beneath the dark sweep of her lashes.

Her eyelids remained closed. 'No.'

'Then what—Eva…?' he prompted sharply as she turned her head away from him. Damn it, he hadn't meant things to go this far—had never intended— 'Eva, speak to me, damn it!' he pressed worriedly as he smoothed the tangle of dark hair back from the dampness of her brow.

'And say what?' she prompted bitterly. 'I came to Paris because I believe your brother seduced my sister, and now—'

'Now I've seduced you,' Michael realised heavily.

'Hardly!' Eva scorned. 'I was there too, Michael. Oh, God, I was there too…!' More tears escaped her lids and fell down her pale cheeks.

'Eva, look at me, damn it!'

She raised her lids slowly, those violet-coloured eyes appearing bruised and slightly haunted as she looked up at him. 'What did we just do?' She groaned. 'What did I just do?' She gave an agonised moan before turning away from him again and curling up into a huddled and defensive ball.

She looked so small and fragile, lying naked on her side with her back turned towards him. Michael could see the vulnerability of her hunched shoulders, the ridges along her slender spine, the gentle curve of her bottom.

'I've only known you a matter of days!' she continued to berate herself disgustedly. 'I don't really know you at all!'

'You know me, Eva,' Michael contradicted gruffly, knowing that it was true. Eva did know him, better than most people did or ever would.

It might have been only days since they first met, but they had been days when Michael knew he had revealed more of himself to Eva than he had to anyone for a very long time. If ever.

Just as he now knew Eva in that same deep and penetrating way...

And not just on a physical level.

He had come to like, not just to desire Eva these past few days, and discovering she was E J Foster, the photographer of 'Harmony', had ensured he had even further insight into exactly who and what Eva Foster was.

She was a woman who felt things deeply. A woman who was honest with herself to the point that she exposed the rawness of her emotions in a way Michael had never been able to do. Or, at least, not for many years.

And, it was that realisation, the honesty and rawness of Eva's emotions, that confirmed the complete nonsense of Michael's initial accusations to her. Much as he did not wish it to be true, he knew that Eva did truly believe that Rafe was the father of her sister's babies.

Just as the honesty of her emotions just now had allowed her to give herself over to him so completely...

Michael could still taste her nectar on his lips as he slowly ran his tongue across them. Just as he could still feel the velvet softness of her skin beneath his hands, and the way she had come alive beneath his caresses, as she made no attempt to hide her responses to him.

Just looking at her now, her skin a pale unblemished ivory in the dim lighting, her hair ebony silk, Michael knew he wanted to touch and taste her like that again!

'Eva—'

'Don't touch me again,' she warned tautly as he placed a gentle hand on her shoulder. He had no need to remove that hand as she scooted across the bed away from him. 'I can't believe I'm lying here stark naked and you're still fully dressed!' she added with self-loathing.

'What does that matter...?' Michael's hand dropped to his side as he fell onto his back against the pillows, watching regretfully between narrowed lids as Eva quickly pulled on her T-shirt, panties and jeans to cover that nakedness before standing up.

'It matters because—' Her hair was a silky tangle about her shoulders, her eyes dark and haunted as she looked across the bed at him. 'You didn't— It was selfish of me to take and not give—'

'Have I said that concerns me?' Michael rasped harshly. No doubt he would pay for that lack of physical release after Eva had left him, but for the moment he was content in having given her pleasure, in having enjoyed her pleasure.

'No...' She gave a dismissive shake of her head as she avoided meeting his gaze before straightening her shoulders determinedly.

'But that doesn't mean I don't feel— It's far too late to move the twins tonight but tomorrow I'll find somewhere else for us all to stay.'

His jaw tightened. 'No.'

Eva's gaze flickered in his direction before quickly moving away again, her cheeks very pale and luminescent in the dimmed lighting. 'What do you mean no...?' she prompted warily.

'Exactly what I said,' Michael bit out grimly as he swung his own legs to the floor before standing up. 'What happened between us tonight—'

'Was a mistake,' she finished tautly, her chin held defensively high as she still refused to look him in the eye. 'You and I both know that,' she added miserably.

Michael wasn't yet sure what tonight was, needed time—and solitude—in which to decide that for himself.

And the repercussions it might have, if any, on what was already a delicate situation...

He did know he didn't like hearing Eva describe it as having been a mistake! 'Let's just both sleep on it, hmm, and then talk again in the morning?' he prompted gruffly.

Eva didn't want to sleep on anything; she wanted to leave this apartment—and Michael—right now. Except she couldn't. Because, for once, the twins were both sleeping peacefully in their cots, and there was no way she was going to disturb them by moving them out of the apartment tonight. After all, where would she go?

How could she have allowed this to happen? *Why* had it happened?

Oh, she had known from the beginning that she found Michael broodingly attractive, that physically he affected her more deeply than any other man she had ever known, but she hadn't realised it was to the extent—to a degree that—

Eva would have laughed scornfully if someone had told her that she and Michael D'Angelo would ever have ended up making love together!

Or, to be more accurate, that Michael would make love to her...

How awkward was that? How *embarrassing* was that?

Eva wanted to curl up in a mortified ball—

again!—just thinking of Michael's lips and hands on her, of the *intimacy* of having his lips and hands on her, *in* her…!

And, much as she tried to avoid admitting it, Eva knew exactly why it had happened.

Eating dinner together these past few evenings, talking together about everything and nothing, had been more relaxing than she could ever have imagined, but it had been looking at the painting and her photograph, both hanging on Michael's bedroom wall, that had pushed their third evening together over into intimacy.

Because in that moment Eva had *seen* Michael for exactly who and what he was. And that who and what he was really wasn't, as she had already suspected it might not be, the coolly remote man he chose to present to the public.

Oh, she might not know the reasons for the veneer Michael had erected on top of his emotions, or when he had done so, but his obvious attachment, to both the painting of the dying rose and her African photograph, had confirmed that it really was the veneer she had suspected it might be.

And behind that veneer were deep and complicated emotions. Emotions that this evening had touched some echoing depth inside Eva, and it was a connection she ultimately hadn't been able to deny. So much so that she'd had no thought of denial when the two of them began to make love.

And the bitter aftermath of that connection was these feelings of disgust at herself and humiliation…

She knew what Rachel, with her complete joy of life, would have said—and that would have been, *Go for it, sis.* And Eva had certainly gone for it. Had she ever! Her body still quivered and quaked in the aftermath of the first orgasm she'd ever experienced. An orgasm that had left her with a lingering hunger for more.

An impossible hunger, when Eva considered her reason for being in Paris in the first place.

Her chin rose. 'I really think it would be for the best if the twins and I were to move out—'

'No,' Michael repeated grimly.

She shot him an irritated frown. 'I don't think that's for you to decide—'

'On the contrary.' Michael straightened determinedly. 'If those two babies are, as you claim, my niece and nephew, then they, and you, will remain here under my protection until I am able to speak to Rafe.'

She arched challenging brows. 'And who's going to protect me from you?'

Michael's jaw tightened. He didn't appreciate the comment, but knew it was deserved, nonetheless. Who was going to protect Eva from him?

Or him from Eva…?

Because Michael had no doubt that if they continued to stay in this apartment together what had happened tonight would almost certainly happen again…

The answering throb in his still engorged shaft, when he was just thinking about making love with Eva again, was confirmation of that!

'Aren't you overestimating your own attraction?' Michael's tone was deliberately scathing as he looked her coldly up and down. But he wished he could take that coldness back as soon as he saw her flinch, and caught the way the shadows darkened beneath those beautiful violet-coloured eyes. However, putting some distance between the two of them, verbally at least, was what he needed to do for now. For both their sakes.

Her mouth tightened. 'Am I?'

'I believe so, yes,' he drawled dismissively. 'Tonight was an…interesting diversion, no doubt brought about by close proximity, but I doubt it will ever be repeated. Now, if you wouldn't mind leaving my bedroom…?' He turned away abruptly. 'Some of us have to go to work in the morning.'

Eva hadn't thought she could feel any more humiliated than she already did, but Michael's cold dismissal of her now proved that she could. And did.

Michael was behaving as if the past half an hour had never happened, was nothing at all like the passionate lover who had so generously gifted her with that incredible, earth-shattering orgasm. And it *had* been a gift, a totally unselfish one.

Just as Michael was now using his fall-back indifference as a defence in his cold dismissal of her…

'Fine,' Eva snapped just as coldly. 'As you say, we'll talk again in the morning. And tomorrow the twins and I will be moving elsewhere until our flight back to England—'

'I've already cancelled your original flight,' Michael informed her arrogantly.

'You've done *what*?' Eva's hands curled into fists at her sides.

He gave an unconcerned shrug. 'I told you that I would.'

'Yes, but— I can't believe— You overbearing, arrogant ass—'

'Language, Eva,' he drawled mockingly.

'—hat,' she finished scathingly. 'How dare you just—? Well, you can just rebook it,' she instructed furiously.

'I don't think so,' he came back mildly.

'Then I will,' she assured forcefully.

'You can try, I suppose,' he nodded unconcernedly. 'But when I spoke to the woman on the booking desk she thanked me for letting her know so promptly, as they have a long waiting list on that flight. So I'm pretty sure you won't be able to get back on that flight, at least.' He looked across at Eva challengingly.

The shortness of Eva's fingernails now dug into the palms of her hands as she clenched them even more tightly. 'You really are an arrogant bast—'

'For the twins' sake I really would suggest you try to curb the tenure of your language,' Michael bit out distantly. 'Also, I believe that children, babies in particular, are very sensitive to the moods of the adults around them, and behave accordingly…?'

Eva had learnt that to her cost over the past three months; if she was in a cranky mood, through lack of sleep or whatever, then the twins tended to pick up on that mood and started to misbehave themselves. And trust the arrogant Michael, who admitted to having no more experience with babies than she had until three months ago, to know that!

Eva wasn't sure that she didn't actually hate him at that moment. She certainly disliked him. Intensely. 'Then I advise you to stay away from me for the rest of our stay here,' she warned fiercely before turning sharply on her heel and leaving the bedroom, not bothering to close the door behind her as she headed for her bedroom that adjoined that of the twins.

Any clearing up still left to do in the kitchen Michael could deal with himself, because Eva had had more than enough of him for one evening!

'Have a croissant, Eva.' Michael held the basket of pastries out to her enticingly as they sat in the dining room eating breakfast. The twins were strapped in the two high chairs he'd had delivered to the apartment the first morning of Eva's stay here, when it had become obvious they were needed, along with a playpen. 'I went out, as usual, this morning to buy them,' he encouraged dryly, having accepted a couple of days ago that his morning routine of strolling out to enjoy a leisurely breakfast at his favourite cafe would have to be put on hold for the duration of Eva and the twins' stay with him. Which didn't mean he couldn't still enjoy the café's delicious croissants, even if he had to go out each morning and buy them!

Breakfast with two six-month-old babies was certainly an experience, as usual half their fruit purée and oats having landed down them rather than in their mouths, as had the milk they were drinking from lidded and spouted cups. They were now gumming their toast more than chewing it with the four teeth they displayed so proudly every time they smiled. Which was often. Enchantingly so.

Michael had quickly learnt not to dress in his suit for work until after breakfast, but instead wore the faded denims from last night and a white T-shirt—currently decorated with some of the twins' breakfast!

But they certainly were a cute pair of babies, Michael allowed ruefully as he politely refused the piece of soggy toast Sophie now offered him.

Their enthusiastically noisy presence also had the added benefit of masking some of the tension that so obviously existed between Eva and Michael this morning.

As expected Michael hadn't slept well, as he first attempted to drive away his still raging erection, an exercise in will power that certainly wasn't helped by the fact that he knew Eva was in another bedroom just that short distance down the hallway.

Another cold shower had helped a little, even if it hadn't succeeded in dispelling that desire for her completely. That had only been achieved when Michael mulled over how best to continue this living arrangement with Eva.

His surprise in realising she was E J Foster, to the extent he had taken her to see her photograph hanging on his bedroom wall, along with Bryn's painting, had meant he had now revealed far too much of his inner self to Eva.

A realisation that now made Michael feel almost as emotionally exposed as Eva no doubt had after the intimacies they had shared the previous night.

The proof of that was in the bristling hostility Eva had shown him this morning when he first entered the kitchen with the bag of pastries, her chilling politeness causing Michael to become equally guarded.

'Thank you.' Eva's gaze avoided meeting his as she now took one of the croissants from the basket.

At least they were still showing a semblance of politeness to each other in front of the twins!

A stilted politeness, maybe, but it was better than the two of them not talking at all, which was what Michael had feared might be the case. Because he had enjoyed Eva's company last night, as he had the previous two nights.

And he had more than enjoyed making love with her!

Despite Eva's chilling demeanour clearly communicating that she would endeavour to ensure it was never repeated.

When Michael was certain that it would…

Mainly because he was having difficulty keeping his hands off her right now!

Eva looked more fragile than ever to him this morning, her eyes darkly shadowed, her face pale, and the tight-fitting denims and purple T-shirt she was wearing today clearly outlining her too-slender figure.

What Eva needed—

Michael was pretty sure that Eva had absolutely no interest in knowing what *he* thought she needed—even if it was something as innocent as several long and uninterrupted nights' sleep, and having someone looking after her for a change.

Michael had certainly been aware of the twins both waking up twice in the night, had even thought of going to their room and taking over while Eva went back to bed, but thought better of it. He knew he had exacerbated the distance between them when his own defences had fallen into place and he had allowed his coldness to hide both his thoughts and feelings.

And so he had remained in his own bedroom last night, aware of Eva talking softly to the twins as she tried to get them both to settle, frustrated at not being able to do anything to help her. Knowing she would reject that offer of help even if he were to make it.

He had something important he needed to discuss with her today, though. But not here, and not when her attention would be divided. 'I would like you to come to the gallery later this morning.'

Eva glanced up from putting honey on her croissant, her gaze wary as she looked across the table at Michael. 'Why?'

'I need to talk to you.'

She frowned. 'We're talking now.'

'And we have a demanding audience,' he pointed out ruefully as Sam gleefully threw his toast across the table.

Eva absently picked up the toast and placed it on the side of her own plate before answering Michael. 'Why at the gallery?'

'Why not?' He shrugged. 'I might even be able to persuade Marie or Pierre to watch the twins while we talk. Pierre has a couple of children of his own.'

She looked at him searchingly, but as usual wasn't able to read anything from Michael's closed expression; he really could be as inscrutable as a sphinx when he chose to be. And he was choosing to be so now.

Eva gave a shake of her head. 'I don't leave the twins with complete strangers.'

'And if I vouch for both Marie and Pierre's trustworthiness?'

Eva gave a humourless smile. 'Believe it or not, I still consider you a stranger as far as the twins are concerned!'

His brows rose almost to his hairline. 'Isn't that a little…short-sighted of you, in the circumstances?'

Eva knew exactly what circumstances Michael was referring to, and she refused, absolutely, to talk about what had happened between the two of them last night. Bad enough it had happened at all, without having a damned post-mortem about it! 'I'm big enough to look after myself. And take the consequences,' she added coolly. 'But I'm much more circumspect when it comes to the welfare of the twins.'

'I wouldn't harm a hair on either of their heads!' He frowned darkly.

'Perhaps.' Eva calmly took a bite of her honey-coated croissant.

'Damn it—'

'Language, Michael,' she reminded him dryly.

He stood up abruptly and began pacing the room, shooting Eva thunderously frowning glances every now and then as he did so, as she calmly finished eating her croissant before attempting to clean away the worst of the debris of the twins' meal.

All the time totally aware of Michael as he prowled restlessly up and down the kitchen.

As far as Eva was concerned last night had been completely out of character for her, and the sooner they both forgot about it, the better she would like it.

And she was still angry with Michael for cancelling her airline tickets without even consulting her. The least he deserved was a little payback for that!

The fact that he looked almost edible this morning wasn't helping her to maintain this distance between them. His hair was slightly tousled from his walk to the bakery, stubble darkening the square thrust of his chin where he hadn't shaved yet this morning, and the white T-shirt and faded denims clearly showed the whipcord strength of that lean and muscled body.

At this rate Eva was going to need another shower—cold this time!—once Michael had left for the gallery!

Just looking at him, her gaze drawn to those sculptured lips that had pleasured her so thoroughly the night before, was enough to make her feel hot and trembling inside. And the throbbing reaction of her breasts and between her thighs, just from looking at him, should be made illegal. As it was, Eva's only defence against that physical attraction was to attempt to keep Michael at a verbal distance. By whatever means.

Besides, it was rather fun winding up the coldly aloof Michael D'Angelo. And goodness knew Eva felt in need of a diversion from the embarrassment she was feeling this morning!

She stood up. 'I have to bath and dress the twins now, and isn't it time you were leaving for the gallery?'

His mouth thinned. 'Don't try to dismiss me, Eva, because it won't work.'

She quirked one dark brow. 'I have no idea what you mean.' She gathered up both Sophie and Sam before turning to face him, a baby held defensively in each arm.

'Archangel,' Michael bit out through clenched teeth. 'Twelve o'clock.'

'I told you—'

'It wasn't a request, Eva,' he assured grimly.

'And I don't react well to orders, so it looks as if we're once again at an impasse…'

Michael held back his temper with effort. A temper that no one else in his acquaintance had ever been able to rouse as easily as Eva now did; even his brother Rafe had to work a little harder at it nowadays! But it seemed that Eva, with just a lift of her eyebrow and a challenge in her voice, was instantly able to annoy the hell out of him.

He drew in a long controlling breath. 'Fine. I'll leave twelve o'clock today free in my diary for you, if you find you can spare the time. How's that?'

Her lips twitched, as if she was holding back a smile. 'I'll see how the morning goes, but I'm not promising anything.'

Michael's tension eased and he held back an answering smile as he saw the satisfied glint in those violet-coloured eyes, and realised the little minx was enjoying this battle of wills between them. 'Good enough.' He nodded. 'Bye, Sophie. Bye, Sam.' He bent down to let the babies kiss him on the cheek in parting as they reached their arms up to him, but made no move to leave as he instead looked down at a suddenly watchful Eva. 'This is all very domesticated. Do I get a goodbye kiss from you too…?'

Her cheeks instantly blazed with colour. 'In your dreams!'

Michael bared his teeth in a smile. 'Believe me, Eva, in my dreams last night you did so much more than just kiss me on the cheek.'

That colour deepened in her cheeks. 'I— You—'

'Yes?' It was Michael's turn to quirk a mocking brow.

'No!' Eva snapped, very aware of the two babies she held in her arms even if Michael wasn't. Although their age obviously ensured there was absolutely no possibility that the twins could understand a word they were saying to each other. That wasn't the point—

Then what was the point?

Eva was too flustered to remember what they had been talking about before, let alone know what the point of *this* conversation was!

She did know that Michael had very neatly turned her little rebellion around on her, and was obviously now enjoying himself at her expense. As she had enjoyed herself at his just minutes earlier!

Ah, yes, now she remembered... 'Have a good day at the office, dear,' she taunted with saccharin sweetness.

Obsidian-black eyes glittered down at her appreciatively. 'Don't work too hard yourself... sweetness,' Michael came back dryly. 'Or forget our date at twelve,' he added challengingly.

'I haven't said I'll be there yet.' Eva frowned. 'And it certainly isn't a date!'

He arched one dark brow. 'We could make it one...'

No, they really couldn't!

Eva might have briefly lost sight last night of her reason for being in Paris, but she would not allow herself to become distracted by this attraction for Michael by doing so again. She certainly didn't want to start thinking of Michael D'Angelo in a romantic way, let alone go out on a *date* with him…

'I don't think so, thank you,' she refused with cool dismissal.

'Pity,' Michael murmured.

Eva gave him a sharp glance, but was totally unable to read anything from the coolness of Michael's expression as he steadily returned that gaze with cool black eyes.

She gave a shake of her head. 'I don't happen to think so.'

Michael gave Eva another searching glance, once again noting the dark shadows beneath her eyes in her too-thin face; Eva really did have the look of a woman this morning whose emotions were delicately balanced on a knife-edge.

Was that so surprising when in the last eighteen months she had lost both her parents and her younger sister, put her career on hold when she had taken over custody and care of her sister's twin babies, and now had the added distress of seeking out the newly married father and asking for his help?

Michael making love to her last night certainly couldn't have helped Eva's already tautly strung emotions!

'I know you were up with the twins a couple of times during the night, so try to get some rest today too, when the twins take their nap, hmm, Eva?' Michael reached up with the intention of gently brushing those shadows beneath her eyes, only for his hand to drop slowly back to his side as Eva flinched back and away from his touch.

Her chin rose challengingly. 'Is that an order or a request?'

'It's a suggestion,' he corrected harshly.

She smiled slightly. 'In that case, I'll take your suggestion under advisement.'

Michael bit back his frustration with her reply, knowing Eva well enough now to realise that if he continued to push the point she would do exactly the opposite. 'You do that,' he bit out tersely, glancing at his watch before looking up at her again. 'I have to go and take a shower now.' He turned sharply on his heel and left the kitchen.

Eva gave a groan as she knew she would carry that image—of Michael's lean and muscled nakedness as he stood beneath the cascade of the hot shower water—around in her head with her all morning!

CHAPTER EIGHT

'I TRUST I'M not…interrupting anything, because by my calculations Eva and I had an appointment ten minutes ago…?'

Eva gave the handsome Pierre an apologetic smile before turning to face the owner of that coldly sarcastic voice. Michael looked every inch the dark and compelling archangel he was named for as he bore down on where she and Pierre were standing talking together in the reception area of the gallery.

And Michael was right—Eva should have been in his office on the third floor ten minutes ago for that twelve o'clock appointment he had suggested over breakfast this morning. She just hadn't been able to resist stopping and talking to his assistant manager, when the charmingly flirtatious Pierre had approached and spoken to her as she entered the gallery.

Or trying to pump him for information on Rachel and Rafe while she was about it!

And she hadn't got very far in that endeavour, had only just got around to casually mentioning her sister's visit to Paris last year, when Michael so rudely interrupted them.

A Michael, eyes glittering like black onyx, nostrils flared, skin taut over the sharpness of his cheekbones, sculptured lips thinned, jaw tensed, who looked absolutely nothing like the sexily tousled, stubble-jawed man she'd had breakfast with this morning, let alone the sensual and sensitive man who had made such exquisite love to her the evening before…

Michael continued to look down coldly at Eva for several more seconds before turning those glacial black eyes on Pierre. 'Shouldn't you have gone to lunch by now?'

Eva drew in a sharp breath at Michael's coldly cutting tone, pretty sure she was responsible. Michael certainly hadn't liked her attempt to question his assistant manager three days ago about whether or not he had remembered Rachel from the previous year, or known anything about Rafe's relationship with her!

'If you remember, you asked that I take care of Miss Foster's children during your appointment with her...?' Pierre now reminded his employer politely.

A nerve pulsed in Michael's tightly clenched jaw. 'Then perhaps you should have offered to do that rather than delay Miss Foster arriving promptly for that appointment.'

Eva had heard quite enough—more than enough, when Pierre's comment made it obvious that Michael was allowing his assistant manager to believe that Sophie and Sam were her children, rather than Rachel and Rafe's!

'It's very kind of you to offer, Pierre.' She turned to give the Frenchman a warm smile as she touched his arm lightly in thanks. 'As you can see, my niece and nephew are both fast asleep at the moment.' She glanced down to where Sophie and Sam slept in the pushchair, their angelic faces revealing none of the mayhem they had caused in Michael's apartment since their arrival.

The playpen and high chairs Michael had ordered to be delivered had helped to ease some of the strain they had suffered that first evening, when she and Michael had needed to chase the twins all over the sitting room in an effort to prevent them from breaking anything. Michael might have admitted to having no previous experience with babies, but he certainly seemed to know what was needed to make life easier for coping with them.

Or, more likely, he was just trying to protect the priceless artefacts and statuary in his apartment!

Whatever his reasoning, Eva had made good use of the high chairs and the playpen, most especially this morning when, after tidying the apartment, she had been able to put the twins safely in the playpen while she changed to go to her twelve o'clock appointment with Michael.

Which she now wished she hadn't bothered to keep, when she could literally *feel* Michael's brooding disapproval of having found her in conversation with the handsome Pierre. A conversation which, frustratingly, hadn't as yet yielded any new information on Rachel and Rafe's relationship…

She ignored Michael's disapproval as she gave Pierre another warm smile. 'You know where I am if you should need me.'

'Of course.' He returned Eva's smile with a

charming one of his own, at the same time as he seemed to be keeping one wary eye on his employer.

Eva's smile noticeably disappeared as she turned to look coldly at Michael. 'Shall we go?' she prompted tersely, not waiting for his reply as she turned and walked off down the marble hallway towards the stairs that would take them to the upper floors.

Michael managed to catch up with Eva enough in three lengthy strides to be able to take a light grasp of her elbow. 'Not here,' he rasped grimly between gritted teeth as she instantly tried to pull away from that hold, his fingers tightening enough to prevent her from doing that without actually bruising her.

Daggers shot out of those violet-coloured eyes as she gave him an angry glance. 'You behaved like an arrogant boor just now to Pierre!'

Yes, he had, Michael accepted, knowing he had been both rude and overly curt towards the younger man. Although he found his reasons for doing so were a little harder to explain…

His morning at the gallery hadn't exactly been his finest hour either, as he had snapped and snarled at everyone he spoke to, almost reducing Marie to tears at one stage with his bad temper. Which had only succeeded in making him feel more annoyed, even as he offered Marie his apologies.

Consequently he had been restlessly pacing his office as he waited for Eva to arrive at twelve o'clock, the minutes ticking by slowly once the clock on his desk reached the noonday hour. By eight minutes past twelve Michael had decided to call his apartment, and when he received no answer to that call had hoped it indicated Eva was on her way here, which was when he had decided to go downstairs and wait for her in Reception.

Reaching the bottom of the marble staircase, and seeing Eva in obviously easy conversation with his charming assistant manager, the two of them then laughing together over one of Pierre's remarks, had made Michael see red.

Or, rather, black…

Because a black tide of displeasure had seemed to sweep over him as he strode purposefully towards the two of them, blocking out all rational or logical thought.

And Michael had absolutely no idea why it was he had reacted in that way...

Except to know he hadn't liked seeing Eva so relaxed and comfortable in another man's company. That same ease of companionship Michael had thought he and Eva had uniquely shared together over these past few days.

Until last night...

Last night had changed everything between them, and Michael hadn't been at all sure that Eva would keep the appointment.

To realise that she had come to the gallery after all, but had delayed going up to his office because she was downstairs in conversation with the too-handsome and too-charming Pierre, had tipped Michael's already precarious mood over into burning displeasure.

He wasn't angry...he was jealous!

Michael drew in a sharp, hissing breath at the thought of what that might mean.

Because he knew, despite the circumstances under which they had met and his initial assumption she was a gold-digger, that he liked Eva... Not only was she beautiful, but she was also intelligent. Her conversation was astute and thought-provoking, and her exquisite photographs, most especially 'Harmony', proved she was also a gifted photographer.

And, after last night, it would be ridiculous of Michael to even attempt to deny he also *desired* her.

Added to which, he also admired her for her emotional resilience, after losing both her parents and her sister in so short a time. And he had no doubt about the deep love she felt for the twins—that love perhaps all the more intense *because* of those other recent family losses?

But to imagine, to think, that he might be starting to have any deeper feelings for Eva was totally unacceptable to him.

It was unacceptable to him to realise he had actually liked, *enjoyed*, these evenings he and Eva had spent together, playing with the twins before feeding and bathing them and then putting them to bed, before the two of them then sat down to enjoy a leisurely dinner together, along with scintillating and intelligent conversation.

So much so that Michael was aware the apartment was going to feel empty, lonely, once Eva and the twins had returned to England…

That last realisation was especially unacceptable to him!

Michael was never lonely—the opposite, in fact. He had always enjoyed his own company, and valued his solitude. As well as the fact that he was answerable to no one in his private life. Business was a different matter, of course, because there he had a responsibility to Gabriel and Rafe, but in his private life he did exactly as he pleased.

And for the past three evenings it had pleased him to be with Eva and the twins...

'Take a seat,' he ground out in invitation once he and Eva had entered his office, closing the door behind them before crossing the room to resume his seat behind the marble desk.

Which was when Michael realised Eva had made no move to do as he asked, his eyes narrowing as he realised how seasonably bright and lovely she looked standing across the room in a sundress of pale lilac, her complexion creamy and smooth, just a pale lip gloss on the full pout of her lips. Her hair was that silky, ebony curtain against the bareness of her lightly tanned shoulders, her legs slender beneath the dress's just-above-the-knee length, flat white sandals on her feet.

His mouth tightened as he felt his shaft throb in recognition of all that unaffected loveliness. 'Eva?'

She still didn't move. 'You really were incredibly rude to Pierre just now—'

'I believe you can safely leave my dealings with my staff to me!' Michael dismissed unyieldingly.

Eva's eyes widened at the unmistakeable coldness in his tone. Could this man, who looked at her with such cool indifference, really be the same one who had made such exquisite love to her last night? Whose hands and lips had touched her everywhere? Who had *tasted* her so intimately?

The answer to those questions was no, of course this wasn't the same man...

This man was every inch the one she had first met, the unapproachable and suspicious Michael D'Angelo, wealthy part-owner of the Archangel galleries, rather than the man who last night had revealed a sensitivity Eva had only guessed might exist.

'You do know that Pierre is married...?'

She frowned across at Michael, not liking the scorn she detected in his expression. 'I had assumed so,' she answered slowly, 'after you told me he has two children of his own...'

Michael nodded abruptly. 'I just thought I would make sure you're aware of that fact.'

'Michael—'

'Eva.'

She gave a shake of her head at the hardness of his tone. 'I don't think I like what you're implying.'

'I'm not implying anything—'

'Oh, I believe that you are!' she said with certainty, sure now more than ever that Michael's obvious distrust of women lay somewhere in his past...

'Won't you please sit down, Eva?' Once again Michael indicated the chair across the desk from his own.

Eva supposed she should be grateful that at least he had said please this time...

She moved slowly forward before perching on the edge of the chair facing Michael across that marble desk, instantly regretting it as she became aware of the way in which it seemed to put more than just the distance of the width of that desk between them, turning this meeting businesslike rather than personal.

As it was meant to?

Of course it was meant to do that, Eva ruefully answered her own question; no doubt Michael was as eager as she was to put their relationship back on an impersonal footing.

She sat up straighter in her chair. 'I assure you, I have absolutely no personal interest in Pierre.'

'And I apologise if you thought I was implying anything else.' Michael nodded brusquely, only too well aware that he *had* been implying something else, that he had totally overreacted to seeing Eva talking with Pierre.

As aware as he was that he refused to acknowledge the reason for that overreaction…

'So, what was it you wanted to discuss with me?' Eva prompted just as briskly.

Michael's brows rose. 'I take it you're not in the mood to exchange pleasantries first?' he drawled dryly. 'Polite enquiries as to whether or not we've both had an enjoyable, or in my case profitable, morning?'

'No,' she dismissed hardly. 'Could we just

get this conversation over with?' she added impatiently as Michael continued to look at her steadily. 'It's getting late, and I want to take the twins to the Eiffel Tower today.'

Michael had been aware that Eva had filled her days by taking the babies around Paris. Where the three of them had been, and the things they had seen, had been part of their conversations over dinner in the evenings.

What surprised him now was the tug he felt to accompany the three of them on this afternoon's excursion...

The Paris Archangel had been open for eight years now, and Michael had spent at least three years of those eight in the French capital in two-to-three-month periods, and he had long grown accustomed to seeing the historical sights of Paris. In fact, he could see the Eiffel Tower from his apartment.

Which would seem to indicate that his interest wasn't in visiting the Eiffel Tower at all but in spending time with Eva and the twins...

His mouth tightened at that realisation. 'I wanted this meeting to take place here at the gallery because I have a business proposition I'd like to discuss with you.'

Eva instantly grew wary as she could think of only one business proposition Michael could possibly have in mind. And after their lapse last night she shouldn't really be surprised. No doubt, having had the morning to think about it, Michael was now eager for her to leave his apartment.

She gave a shake of her head. 'I don't believe you should think about paying me off until after we've spoken to your brother—'

'We aren't speaking to Rafe, Eva, I am,' Michael corrected harshly as he straightened abruptly. 'And I have no intention of paying you off, as you put it, when we haven't yet established that Rafe is the father of your sister's children!'

Eva felt the flush of anger in her cheeks at his continued doubting of her claim; Rachel might have been many things, immature and irresponsible being two of them, but she certainly hadn't been a liar, and before she died she had clearly told Eva that Rafe D'Angelo was the father of the twins. 'I will speak to your brother myself—'

'That's not going to happen,' Michael assured her grimly.

Eva's eyes widened at the certainty in his voice. 'You may be a rich and powerful man, Michael, but you can't prevent me from seeing and talking to Rafe if I want to. And I do,' she added determinedly.

'This has nothing to do with how rich or how powerful I may or may not be.' He sighed heavily. 'Eva, don't you think it would be…kinder to Nina, Rafe's wife, if I were the one to talk to him? Privately,' he added softly.

The blush deepened in Eva's cheeks at the quiet rebuke she could hear in Michael's voice. 'If I had wanted to make things unpleasant for Rafe's wife then I would already have done so. Instead I agreed to wait until they return from their honeymoon before talking to him.'

She had, Michael accepted. Because he had asked her to do so.

'All I want to do is get to the truth,' Eva added softly.

'As do I.' Michael nodded tersely. 'And I believe we will achieve that more…discreetly, if I'm the one who talks to Rafe.'

Although how the hell Michael was even going to begin to broach the subject of Rachel Foster to his newly married brother, let alone whether or not Rafe could be the father of her twin babies, he had no idea!

Even if Rafe denied it, as Michael seriously expected him to do—his brother might have been something of a playboy before he met and fell in love with Nina, but he certainly hadn't been irresponsible enough not to have used contraception in all of his previous relationships—then he had no doubt that Eva would demand blood tests in order to prove that denial, further complicating an already delicate situation.

Michael had never seen Rafe as happy as he had been since he fell in love with Nina, and the thought of Eva's accusations of Rafe's paternity and the damage it might cause to his brother's relationship with Nina, made Michael feel physically ill.

But at the same time he felt empathy for Eva's situation.

He had come to know Eva well enough to know she wasn't doing any of this out of spite or malice, or any sense of revenge, or with the intention of blackmailing Rafe for money, that she truly was just finding it impossible to financially care for Sophie and Sam, and needed their father's help to continue doing so. Understandably so, when caring for the twins meant Eva could no longer work at her chosen profession, and the day-to-day care of two babies was an expensive business.

Which left Michael feeling damned if he did and damned if he didn't.

And the stiffness of Eva's pride told him she would never accept financial help from him, no matter what the outcome of his conversation with Rafe.

'I really didn't ask you here to talk about any of that,' he dismissed evenly.

Eva sighed. 'Then why did you ask me here?'

His mouth thinned at the weariness of her tone. 'As I said, I have a business proposition to put to you—it doesn't involve paying anyone off!' he bit out as he saw she was about to refuse a second time.

Eva looked at him searchingly for several long tense seconds, but as usual she could read none of Michael's thoughts from his closed expression. 'Then what does it involve…?' she finally prompted slowly, suspiciously.

'Your Tibetan photographs.'

She blinked her surprise at his answer. 'Sorry?'

Michael shrugged. 'You mentioned you had brought back enough photographs of Tibet from your visit there last year for a second exhibition?'

'Yes…'

'And you already know that I'm a great admirer of E J Foster's work,' he drawled ruefully.

'Yes…' Eva felt the warmth enter her cheeks at the memory of exactly how she knew that. Of exactly where she had been, where they had both been, when she had discovered that. And the intimacies that had followed…

Michael nodded. 'I'm also—conveniently,' he added dryly, 'one of the owners of a collection of international art galleries and auction houses.'

'Yes…'

He eyed her impatiently. 'Is that "yes" spoken in that less than trusting way going to be your only contribution to this conversation?'

'That depends…'

Those onyx-black eyes narrowed guardedly. 'On what?'

'On exactly where this conversation is going!' Eva wasn't sure what else she could say, when she had no idea yet what Michael was leading up to with this conversation. An idea had occurred to her, certainly, but it was such a fantastically unrealistic one it couldn't possibly be right.

No way Michael would ever want, ever think of suggesting, that she—that E J Foster—consider having an exhibition of her Tibetan photographs in one of the three prestigious Archangel galleries!

No, of course Michael wasn't suggesting that. It would be madness on Eva's part to even think that he might—

'What I'm proposing, Eva,' Michael bit out evenly, 'is that you consider exhibiting a selection of E J Foster's Tibetan photographs in the Archangel gallery of your choice.'

CHAPTER NINE

EVA'S EYES WENT wide with disbelief as she continued to stare across the desk at Michael for several long seconds, before another emotion took its place, her eyes glittering with anger as she stood up abruptly, a flush to her cheeks now. 'How could you?' she accused emotionally, trembling hands clenching into fists at her sides, angry tears blurring her vision. 'I knew from the moment I met you that you were a hard, cold man—'

'Eva—'

'—who didn't believe a word I was saying to you—'

'Eva!'

'—but even knowing that,' she continued as those tears began to fall hotly down her cheeks, 'I didn't think even you would ever be so deliberately cruel.'

'Damn it, don't cry…!' Michael stood up to

move quickly out from behind his desk before reaching out for her.

'Don't touch me,' Eva warned through numbed lips even as she stepped away to evade his grasp. 'How could you, Michael? How could you *be* so cruel? How could you…?' she choked again as she raised her hands to bury her face in them, the scalding-hot tears falling between her fingers.

'Damn it, Eva…!'

Eva had no fight left inside her to be able to pull away a second time as Michael drew her firmly into his arms, her salty tears instantly dampening the pristine whiteness of his silk shirt as one of his hands cupped the back of her head and held her gently to his chest.

She *knew* none of this could be easy for Michael—any easier than it had all been for her when she first learnt of Rachel's pregnancy and illness—and she empathised with the shock he must have felt when she had turned up at the gallery with the twins.

Yes, Eva could sympathise, but this—this was uncalled for. Cruel, as she had already said, when Eva ached inside, longed for nothing more than to be able to continue with her career, and to exhibit more of her photographs.

The very carrot Michael was now dangling so temptingly in front of her nose...

But she would never, could never take that carrot, when the price might endanger the twins' future!

Michael was at a complete loss to know what to do with the silently sobbing Eva as he continued to hold her in his arms.

Not sure whether he felt angry or hurt at Eva's accusation of 'I didn't think even you would ever be so deliberately cruel...'

Even him?

What did that mean? That Eva believed him to be cold and hard obviously, but that she also hadn't believed that coldness and hardness to be deep enough, ingrained enough, for him to treat her cruelly?

Bad enough in itself, but Michael had no idea what cruelty Eva was referring to.

He had thought she would be pleased with his proposition.

What the hell sort of cruelty could there possibly be in his having invited her to exhibit her latest photographs in one of the Archangel galleries—?

Michael tensed as the answer hit him squarely between the eyes. 'Eva, do you think my offer of the exhibition is another way of me paying you off...?' he grated slowly. 'As in, your silence about Rafe in exchange for exhibiting your photographs at Archangel?'

'What else could it be?' She sniffled miserably as she attempted to mop up some of the tears dampening Michael's chest.

What else indeed...?

Michael now knew exactly what emotion he was feeling! 'You know, Eva,' he bit out with steely calm, 'I knew, from the moment I met *you*, that you could be impetuous and outspoken, but I hadn't realised until now that you could also be so damned insulting as to accuse me of blackmailing you into silence!'

'You don't like the accusation any more than I did...'

No, he didn't. Because he had believed, after last night, that Eva was learning to trust him. As much as he now trusted her...?

Whatever he had believed he had been wrong, damn it!

He reached up to grasp her arms and hold her away from him as he looked down at her with glittering black eyes. 'Look at me, Eva,' he instructed harshly as she continued to look down at that damp patch on his shirt. 'I said, look at me, damn it!' he repeated hardly.

She raised wet dark lashes to look up at him with eyes of a deep and bruised purple, her face deathly pale. 'I never—I didn't use the word blackmail...'

'You didn't need to!' A nerve pulsed in Michael's tightly clenched jaw. 'It was right there alongside your other accusations...coldness and cruelty.' He released her arms to walk across to stand in front of the floor-to-ceiling windows looking out onto the Champs Élysées, not seeing any of the grandness of the wide avenue. 'I thought you had come to know me better than that, Eva. Believed we had reached an understanding— Oh, to hell with what I believed; why should you be any different from every other bloody woman?' he added bleakly. 'I think you should leave now, before one or both of us says something else we're going to regret.'

Eva stared across at Michael, the rigidity of his stance unmistakeable: tensed shoulders, back stiff and straight, hands thrust into the pockets of his tailored trousers, feet slightly parted.

He looked…chillingly unapproachable. Because of the things she had said? Because she had assumed that his offer was an attempt on his part to blackmail her into silence—?

When she put it as bluntly as that it did sound pretty awful, Eva realised with a pained wince. Especially when she now realised Michael hadn't actually said that…

What had he said, exactly?

That he wanted to offer her, as E J Foster, the opportunity to exhibit her Tibetan photographs at the Archangel gallery of her choice.

There had been no mention in that offer of anything to do with the twins, or Rafe, or anything else to do with that situation, only that it was a business proposition.

Did that mean Michael really had just been offering her the chance to exhibit her photographs with no strings or conditions attached?

Eva moistened her lips with the tip of her tongue before speaking again, her voice gruff from the tears she had shed. 'If I was mistaken—'

'Oh, you were!' he assured grimly.

Eva wasn't in the least encouraged by the coldness of Michael's voice or the way he kept his back turned towards her as he continued to look out onto the busy Champs Élysées. 'Then I apologise,' she finished lamely.

'Big of you!' Michael did turn around now, his expression as coldly scathing as his tone as those black eyes raked over her with merciless intensity. 'I don't believe I can talk about this any more just now, Eva,' he finally bit out with cold dismissal.

'You have another appointment...?'

'No, I just can't—I think it best if we don't discuss this any further right now,' he answered uncompromisingly.

Eva winced as she heard the cold implacability in Michael's tone.

He really was icily, chillingly, furious. Rightly so, if her accusation really had been so far off the mark! 'Then later? At ho—er—at your apartment?' She grimaced, her cheeks blazing hotly at the slip of having almost called Michael's apartment 'home'.

Its luxurious impersonality barely rendered it as being Michael's Parisian home, let alone her own!

His mouth twisted derisively as he obviously realised the reason for her embarrassed blush. 'Yes, perhaps we'll talk about this again later at the apartment.'

Eva frowned. 'Perhaps…?'

He drew in a deep and even breath, as if fighting to maintain control of his temper. 'At this point in time I'm not sure there's anything left for us to discuss.' He shrugged. 'There's always a chance I might feel differently about it later on today.'

And that, Eva acknowledged heavily, was the end of the subject for now, as far as Michael was concerned. And, if his offer really had just been the business proposition he'd said it was, then she couldn't exactly blame him for feeling that way!

She had, Eva realised, with a few choice words and her accusing tears, succeeded in totally destroying the shaky truce that had slowly been growing between the two of them, but had already been so severely tested by the intimacies they had shared the night before.

'I'll go now,' she said abruptly. 'I— What time should I expect you back for dinner?'

Michael's mouth twisted with derision as he realised Eva had carefully avoided referring to his apartment as 'home' a second time.

'I have absolutely no idea,' he dismissed flatly, not sure it was a good idea for him to join Eva at the apartment for dinner this evening at all.

Hadn't he decided earlier that having Eva and the twins at the apartment was becoming just a little too cosy, too domesticated for comfort? *His* comfort?

A cosiness and domesticity Michael realised he was in no mood for this evening, after Eva's distrust of him. 'I could be late, so just order something in for yourself,' he added coolly as he resumed his seat behind his desk. 'Could you please send Marie in on your way out...?' he added distractedly as he pulled the proofs for the next Parisian Archangel catalogue towards him and began to read through them.

Eva took one last lingering look at Michael, as

he bent over some papers lying on the top of his desk, before leaving, knowing herself well and truly dismissed...

The digital clock on Eva's bedside table read eleven fifty-one in the darkness of the bedroom when she heard Michael use his key to enter the otherwise silent apartment. Listening intently, she heard him drop his key into the glass bowl on the table in the hallway alongside the spare key he had given her some days ago, followed by the soft thud of his briefcase as he placed it beneath that table, before moving quietly to the kitchen.

And Eva was aware of him making every single one of those soft movements—because she had left her bedroom door slightly open for just that purpose when she crawled miserably into bed a couple of hours ago!

After what had been a long and awful afternoon and evening as far as Eva was concerned. The twins, having predictably picked up on her tension when she had returned downstairs to collect them from Pierre, had then proceeded to be cranky and fretful all afternoon. And they hadn't improved when they all returned to the apartment, throwing food at each other when Eva fed them their tea, and splashing water over each other when she bathed them.

Eva had given a sigh of relief when it came time to put them in their separate cots for the night!

Only to then find she had the rest of the long and lonely evening stretching out in front of her...

Michael hadn't returned by nine o'clock, and Eva had felt too despondent to order any food in for her own dinner, deciding to settle for making some toast instead, and ending up feeling quite sorry for herself as she sat down alone in the quiet of the kitchen to eat it.

She had never been a particularly social person, had shared accommodation at university, but had preferred the privacy of her own space after she moved to London. The twins had shattered that privacy three months ago, of course, but even so Eva had never felt lonely, just exhausted, once she had put the babies to bed for the night.

She had been very aware of feeling lonely this evening...

Because, in just a very short space of time, Eva knew she had become accustomed to spending her evenings with Michael. Had come to appreciate, to enjoy, their quiet dinners together, their conversation, and even their silences had seemed companionable rather than awkward.

This evening there had just been a yawning great hole of loneliness where Michael should have been.

Leaving Eva with hours and hours to wonder where he was and what he was doing…

She very much doubted he had been at a business meeting all these hours, so he had probably spent the evening socially. With another woman.

Another woman…?

That would seem to imply that Eva thought of herself as being a woman Michael was involved with. Which she didn't—did she…?

Of course she didn't! That would just be asking for trouble.

She'd never thought to ask, and Michael hadn't volunteered the information either, as to whether or not he had a woman currently in his life.

But of course there would be!

How could Eva have been stupid enough not to have realised that earlier? Michael was a darkly gorgeous and complex man, and an experienced and exquisite lover, added to which he was seriously wealthy, and Eva had no doubt there was sure to be some other woman currently appreciating all three of those highly attractive qualities.

Had that other woman been appreciating those qualities this evening?

It really was none of her business, Eva accepted heavily. Just because Michael had made love to her last night didn't give her any right to feel hurt, or jealous, because he was spending the evening with another woman.

Except Eva knew that she did…

She felt incredibly hurt just thinking about it. And she felt jealous because—because Eva had realised, as she sat alone in Michael's apartment this evening, waiting for him to come home, that she had been falling in love with him!

He was totally the wrong man, and it was totally the wrong time for her to fall in love with anyone, and yet Eva knew that was exactly what she had done. She was in love with Michael D'Angelo, the very last man who would ever allow himself to fall in love with her, the woman accusing his brother of fathering her niece and nephew.

And quite how she was going to continue staying on at this apartment with Michael, until Rafe returned from his honeymoon, knowing that she was in love with him, Eva had absolutely no idea. She—

'Eva...?'

Every part of Eva froze as she realised that, while she had been lying here agonising over the fact that she had fallen in love with Michael—a man she could never have, and who would never allow himself to feel the same way about her—he had obviously left the kitchen and walked down the hallway, seen her bedroom door was slightly ajar, and decided to see if she was still awake.

'It's no use pretending to be asleep, Eva, because I could actually feel your recriminating thoughts pounding at me just now through the bedroom wall.'

'Recriminating?' Eva repeated challengingly as she gave up all pretence of being asleep. She sat up abruptly in the bed, uncaring that she was only wearing a soft white cotton camisole top and loose boxers, as she frowned across at Michael's silhouette in her now fully open bedroom door-way. 'I don't have the right to feel that way,' she continued sharply, 'when I'm so obviously an unwanted guest in your apartment!'

'I think what happened between us last night totally disproves part of that statement,' Michael came back wearily, at the same time as he ran a distracted hand through his thick hair, his head pounding painfully with the headache he'd suffered for the past two hours.

A headache certainly not helped by the sight of Eva wearing a barely there top, her hair a glossy ebony tangle about her bare shoulders, as the blood pounded hotly through his veins in response to her.

'You—'

'Have you eaten?'

'I— No, not really.' Eva was taken aback by the abrupt change of subject. 'Just a piece of toast,' she added softly.

Michael nodded abruptly. 'I'm about to go back to the kitchen and make myself an omelette, if you would care to join me?'

'You haven't eaten this evening either?'

'No,' he sighed.

'I assumed you would have been out for dinner…?'

He shook his head. 'I've been working in my office all evening.'

Eva fought to hold back the elation she felt at hearing this. 'I thought you couldn't cook.'

'An omelette isn't cooking,' he assured dryly. 'And I didn't say I couldn't cook, only that I don't.'

'Semantics.' Eva nodded ruefully, feeling more light-hearted than she had all evening. Because she now knew that Michael hadn't been out with another woman this evening, after all...

'Yes or no to the omelette, Eva?' Michael was hoping that food might help relieve some of his pounding headache. Although, with Eva looking so sexily tousled, he doubted it very much as his shaft now pounded, thickened and hardened, to the same rhythm of that pulsing headache...!

'Yes.' She threw back the bedclothes with the obvious intention of getting out of bed.

Giving Michael a clear view of the silky bare legs she swung to the carpeted floor before she stood up to pick up her robe from the chair, that short walk revealing that she wore a loose pair of black boxers to sleep in along with that barely there white top.

Michael turned away abruptly as his hardened

shaft pulsed eagerly in response. 'I'll see you in the kitchen in a few minutes.'

'I'm just—'

Michael didn't linger in the doorway to hear what else Eva was going to say as he turned sharply on his heel and returned to the kitchen, just that brief glimpse of her in that sexy top and boxers enough to set his blood pounding even harder. He moved grim-faced about the kitchen collecting up the ingredients for their omelettes.

'Did you have an enjoyable evening working?' Eva prompted huskily as she quietly entered the kitchen to stand near the door watching as Michael whisked the eggs in a bowl.

'No.' He kept his back towards her. 'You?'

'No.'

'Why not? Were the twins difficult?' Michael didn't need to glance away from tipping the egg mixture into the pan to be achingly aware of Eva's every move as she crossed the kitchen to sit down on one of the chairs about the table in the centre of the room.

He could smell her, that perfume that was uniquely Eva: a mixture of citrus and hot earthy woman.

'A little. But that wasn't it. I—I've been…un-happy, about the way we parted earlier,' she admitted huskily.

Michael continued to keep his back to her as he closed his eyes, counting slowly to ten as he willed himself not to respond to that admission. If their argument this afternoon, the things Eva had said to him, had shown him nothing else, then it had convinced Michael that it was in the best interest of both of them if he avoided Eva's company in future.

And so he had stayed away from the apartment this evening, filling those hours with work, uninterested in eating dinner as he kept himself busy, and resulting in his now having this blinding headache.

He faltered slightly as he carried the first laden plate over to the table as he saw Eva looked more luscious than ever. 'Eat,' he instructed tersely as he placed the plate of hot food on the table in front of her, before turning sharply away to return to the hob to cook his own omelette.

'Mmm, this is really good,' she murmured appreciatively seconds later.

Michael made a gruff noise of acknowledgement, having no appetite for his own omelette now but tipping it out of the pan and onto the plate anyway before walking over to sit opposite Eva at the wooden table.

If anything Eva felt more miserable now than she had earlier this evening.

She had felt briefly happy at knowing he had spent the evening at his office rather than going out, but that had now been replaced by the fact that at least before she had only been able to guess at the anger Michael felt towards her. Being here with him now, able to see and feel that displeasure firsthand, was unbearable!

So much so that Eva could only push the rest of her omelette uninterestedly about her plate, Michael appearing to do the same with his as the minutes slowly passed with the marked ticking of the kitchen clock. They brooded in silence, Eva because she simply couldn't think of anything to say, and Michael because he obviously just didn't have anything he wanted to say to her...

Eva lowered her lashes and looked down at the table as she heard Michael's chair scrape on the tiled floor, so miserable now she was totally unable to prevent the tears from falling softly down her cheeks; damn it, she had cried more in the last few days than she had for months!

'Eva…?' Michael's legs appeared beside her first, and then his chest and face as he came down onto his haunches to look up at her bowed head. 'Why are you crying…?' he prompted softly as one of his hands moved up and his fingertips gently smoothed those tears from her cheeks.

'This time?' Eva asked.

He gave a rueful smile. 'My offer of an exhibition of your work at one of the Archangel galleries still stands, Eva.'

Her gaze flicked up to his in surprise. 'It does?'

Michael nodded. 'No conditions. Absolutely no strings attached,' he added grimly.

Eva ran her tongue over her lips. 'I— That's very generous of you after the things I said to you earlier.'

'You think?' He arched dark and mocking brows. 'I'm sure my brothers would both assure you that I'm just using good business sense by securing the next E J Foster photographic exhibition for our galleries.'

Eva's heart plummeted. Because she had

wanted, hoped, that Michael having repeated his earlier offer meant he had forgiven her for the things she had said. 'I see.'

'Somehow I doubt that.' Michael's dark gaze roamed freely over her make-up-free face as he gently smoothed the hair back from her temple. 'I've been fighting coming home and doing this all evening, Eva,' he groaned huskily, 'but now that I'm here with you again, I can't fight it any longer!'

She swallowed. 'This…?'

'This!' One of his hands captured both of hers before he straightened abruptly, taking Eva with him. 'I want to make love to you,' he grated huskily. 'Do you want me in the same way?'

The best thing to do, the sensible thing to do, would be for Eva to say no, to just walk away and go back to her bedroom and close the door behind her; she had absolutely no doubt that Michael would accept the closing of that door as her final answer.

That was the sensible thing to do.

'Yes.' Eva didn't even attempt to qualify that one-word answer by adding anything else.

She did want Michael. Madly. Passionately.

And if tonight was all she was going to have of him then she was going to take it!

CHAPTER TEN

MICHAEL DREW IN a harshly ragged breath at hearing Eva answer him with her usual straight-forwardness. He should have expected it of her, of course, but he had hardly dared to hope that might be her answer…

'My bedroom or yours?' he prompted gruffly as his arms moved possessively about her waist, the headache that had been plaguing him all evening having miraculously disappeared.

'Does it matter?' Her hands slid slowly up his waistcoat and shirt-covered chest to his shoulders, before her fingers moved to become entangled in the hair at his nape.

No, it didn't matter where, Michael accepted, all that mattered at this moment was making love with Eva, a need that he was only too well aware had consumed his every waking moment since last night.

'Whichever bedroom it is I think you're a little overdressed for what we have in mind!' Eva teased huskily.

The two of them must look slightly ludicrous, Michael accepted ruefully; Eva was dressed in her nightclothes, and he was still wearing the white silk shirt, waistcoat and trousers of the formal three-piece suit he had worn to work that morning, his jacket draped over the back of one of the kitchen chairs.

'Shower first,' he announced firmly. 'Some of us have been working all day and all evening!' He swung Eva easily up into his arms.

'Whoa!' She laughed, her arms moving about his neck so that she could hold on tightly as Michael walked out of the kitchen with her in his arms and then down the hallway to his bedroom.

He didn't so much as hesitate outside the door but instead just kicked it open and strode inside the darkened room and straight through to the adjoining bathroom.

Eva's eyes widened. 'I get to watch you shower?'

'You get to join me in the shower,' Michael corrected gruffly.

'I've already taken a shower this evening,' Eva

protested laughingly as Michael sat her down on top of the vanity unit before moving to switch on the light and turn on the water, the smoky glass-sided shower so large it took up almost half of the spacious and opulently appointed bathroom. The tiles on the walls and floor were terracotta and cream, with gold fittings in the shower and double sink, with half a dozen fluffy gold-coloured towels on the warmer.

'Not with me you haven't,' Michael said with satisfaction as he turned, his dark gaze holding hers captive as he took off his tie before unbuttoning his waistcoat and taking that off too. He threw both items onto the narrow marble bench running along one of the walls.

Eva was fascinated, watching Michael as he slowly unfastened his shirt before slipping that off his shoulders and down his arms. Muscles rippled in his tanned chest and back as the shirt joined the rapidly growing pile of his clothes. She couldn't think as far ahead as the shower he was obviously suggesting they take together.

His torso was…magnificent. Olive skinned, silky dark hair down the centre of his chest, lean and muscled, with not an ounce of superfluous flesh anywhere, and—

Eva's breath caught in her throat as Michael's hands moved to the fastening on his trousers before lowering the zip, the colour burning her cheeks as her gaze moved quickly back up to his face.

'Doesn't this seem fair to you after last night...?' he prompted gruffly.

When Eva had been completely naked and Michael had remained fully dressed...

'Yes,' she confirmed huskily, grateful for what he was doing, and determined not to avert her gaze as Michael first dispensed with his shoes and socks before removing his trousers too Now he wore only a pair of black boxers that hugged his sculpted hips and thighs above long and muscled legs.

Black hip-hugging boxers that also did very little to hide the lengthy bulge of his arousal!

And then it wasn't hidden any more as Michael stood completely naked in front of her, his arousal surging up towards his taut abdomen.

Michael was gorgeous in his nakedness.

Unashamedly, blatantly, beautifully gorgeous!

Eva was completely unaware that she was running her tongue slowly over her lips as the heat of her gaze feasted on all that blatant olive-skinned maleness. His thick and pulsing shaft seeming to lengthen and thicken even more as she gazed her fill.

'God, Eva…!'

Her gaze flickered up to Michael's face as she heard the husky longing in his voice at his reaction to having the heat of her gaze on him. He breathed shallowly, his whole body tense, hands clenched into fists at his sides, as if he was waiting to see what she would do next.

Eva knew what she wanted to do—

What she was going to do!

Last night she had longed to touch and taste Michael in the same intimate way he had touched and tasted her. In the way his aroused nakedness now invited her to touch and taste him…

Eva's gaze held Michael's as she slowly slid down from her seat on top of the vanity unit before walking barefoot across the heated tiles towards him. Her gaze lowered as she came to a halt just inches away from him and she ran the fingertips of both hands lightly across his chest and stomach, before curling them about the long and silken length of his shaft.

'Eva…!' He gave a strangulated groan, hands clenching into fists at his sides even as his hips thrust up instinctively forward into those encircling fingers.

She dropped gently to her knees in front of him onto the heated tiles, once again running her tongue across her lips. She brushed the soft pad of her thumb over his moistened tip and, holding his gaze with hers, she brought her thumb to her mouth.

He tasted delicious, slightly salty, with an underlying addictive sweetness that she suspected was uniquely Michael.

Whatever it was she wanted to taste more of him, breathing softly against that sensitive head as she moved closer before parting her lips and taking him completely into her mouth.

'Eva, I'm not sure I can— Dear sweet heaven!' Michael groaned in ecstasy as Eva took even more of him inside the heat of her mouth, her tongue an erotic rasp as it flattened over the sensitive head.

She repeated the same caress over and over

again, licking, lapping, even as she sucked him deeper and then deeper still, and all the time her fingers clasped tightly about the inches she couldn't manage, pumping in the same rhythm, taking the fullness of him a little further each time until he felt the back of her throat caressing, stroking that sensitive tip.

'No more, Eva…!' Michael's hands moved out to grasp her shoulders, his eyes burning down into hers as she looked up at him without releasing him, her eyes deep purple between silky dark lashes. 'I'm not going to last if you don't stop now.' He drew in a deep and ragged breath as he once again felt the caressing sweep of her tongue. 'I want to be inside you when I come,' he bit out between gritted teeth, his control now balanced on a knife's edge as he felt himself torn between the longing to allow Eva to continue, to just give in to the pleasure of her caressing mouth and hands until he came, exploding into that welcoming heat, and the desire he also felt to be buried deep inside her when that happened. 'Please, Eva…!' he groaned achingly.

Her shoulders relaxed beneath his hands as she sat back slightly on her haunches, lips sliding slowly, reluctantly, back along the length of his shaft until she released him, eyes dark and sultry as she looked up at him, her full lips red and slightly pouting.

Michael chuckled huskily at the reproachful look in Eva's eyes as his hands moved beneath her elbows and drew her up slowly until she stood in front of him. 'I assure you, stopping you hurt me a lot more than it did you!' He tapped her playfully on the end of her nose, groaning softly as he watched her run her tongue slowly over her lips as she enjoyed the lingering taste of him, first the top one, then the lower one, humming softly in her throat as she did so, her eyes half closed in pleasure.

Eva hadn't wanted to stop, had felt totally aroused just from kissing and tasting Michael, her breasts aching with that arousal, between her thighs hot and moist, the lips there swollen with her need, her hunger to take him deep inside her.

And if she had ever had any doubts about Michael 'melting' during lovemaking then she didn't now—he was as on fire for her as she was for him!

She trembled slightly as Michael now slipped

the robe from her shoulders and let it fall to the tiled floor before gazing down at her round breasts as they thrust against the thin material of her camisole. Eva had no need to look down to know that her tingling nipples were aroused to the size of plump berries. Just as her core was also plump and wet. So very wet, and even hotter with need…

Michael didn't think he'd ever seen anything as sexy as Eva looked right now in the simple white camisole top and those black boxer shorts! More sexy, more desirable, than any female model ever could have done displaying the skimpiest of satin and lace underwear!

There was just something so damned beautiful, so utterly feminine in the way the male boxers sat low on her slim hips, and her thin camisole revealed her peaked nipples.

He held her gaze with his as he reached down and lifted that top up and over her head, dropping it to the tiled floor with her robe as he proceeded to drink his fill of those perfect and naked breasts. Full and sloping globes that he already knew fitted perfectly into his hands, tipped with ripe nipples he couldn't wait to taste again.

He lowered his head slowly to lingeringly kiss each one as he hooked his fingers into the top of her boxers and slid them down her hips and thighs, able to smell the sweet lure of Eva's arousal as he dropped to his knees in front of her and buried his face in her ebony curls.

'No fair!' Eva protested huskily even as she stepped away from him. 'If you won't then neither will I,' she explained huskily as Michael looked up at her with hot, questioning eyes. 'Besides, the room is filling up with steam from the shower running, and think of all the water we're wasting!'

'This isn't a time for practicality, Eva!' Michael chuckled indulgently even as he picked her up in his arms and carried her over to the glass-sided shower.

'You like doing that, don't you—? Michael!' Eva gasped in protest as he stepped beneath the hot spray of the shower with her still in his arms, soaking them both in seconds.

Michael looked down at her, rivulets of water cascading over his dark, silky hair and down his body. 'I like doing this even more,' he assured huskily, kissing her hungrily as he allowed her body to slide down the length of his.

Eva felt completely dazed with pleasure by the time Michael broke the kiss and reached for the shower gel, his gaze holding hers as he began to wash and caress every inch of her, not a single part of her left untouched by the sureness of those arousing hands. 'My turn,' she murmured softly as she proceeded to wash him in the same intimate way.

Michael withstood those deliberately arousing caresses for as long as he could before finally wresting the shower gel from Eva's hands and placing it back on the shelf, turning off the cascading water before picking Eva up in his arms once again and striding out of the shower unit, across the heated tiles, and into his adjoining bedroom, all without collecting any of the fluffy gold towels on the warmer.

'We'll make the bed all wet!' Eva's protest was only half-hearted as Michael placed her down on top of the bedcovers before quickly joining her.

'Who cares?' Michael grated as he kissed the long column of her silky throat before turning his attention to those full and tempting breasts, the slope of her abdomen, and then lower still.

'I need you inside me now, Michael,' Eva groaned achingly just minutes later, her face flushed with arousal, those purple eyes dark with longing. 'Please!' She looked down at him plead- ingly.

Michael could still taste Eva as he slowly moved to lie between her parted thighs before positioning himself at her entrance, his hands on her hips, his gaze holding her fevered one as he forced himself to enter her slowly, inch by silken inch.

He gritted his teeth in an effort to maintain con- trol as the heat of her channel surrounded him, claimed him, drawing him in deeper, and then deeper still as her legs moved up about his thighs, her feet touching his lower back as she arched up and into him, taking him deeper, deeper and deeper until Michael knew he touched the very heart of her.

Eva groaned with pleasure as Michael's mouth claimed hers even as his shaft filled her com- pletely, stretching her as he began to slowly thrust in and out. Her hands clung to his shoulders as her thighs lifted to meet each of those thrusts, even as Eva lost herself in the wonder of the possession of his tongue thrusting into the heat of her mouth in the same erotic rhythm, taking her pleasure higher, wilder, as she met and matched each of those firm thrusts.

Her groans grew more fevered as Michael broke the kiss to claim one of her nipples, suckling deeply, his tongue an arousing rasp against that sensitive flesh, teeth biting as Eva's groans grew throatily breathier.

'Michael…!' she finally cried out, pleading, as the pleasure grew to an almost unbearable intensity as his thrusts grew fiercer, wilder still, faster, her nails digging into his flesh as the pleasure took her higher, and then higher, until it seemed that Michael held her suspended on that plateau of wild pleasure.

Her head thrashed from side to side on the pillows, her breath a broken sob before she cried out, screamed, as the dam broke inside her and the pleasure coursed hotly into and through every inch of her at the same time as Michael cried out, back arching, head thrown back, and she felt the heat of his hot release pumping into her again and again as she continued to climax.

Minutes, hours later, the last of the pleasure finally spent, only the lingering sensitivity and warmth of feeling remained. The sound of their ragged breathing filled the still, heavy air that now surrounded them.

Eva had never known anything—had never experienced anything so—had never realised that anything could be so—

'Dear God, what have I done…?' Michael suddenly groaned, taking his full weight on his elbows as he raised his head from her throat to look down at her. 'I'm so sorry, Eva. I didn't—I never meant things to go as far as this!'

Eva looked up at him blankly, too befuddled still, too satiated, from the intensity of their lovemaking, to be able to make sense of what he was saying.

Michael's expression was grim, a bleakness in the darkness of his eyes as he looked down at her searchingly for several long seconds before shaking his head. 'I'm really sorry, Eva,' he bit out gruffly. 'That was—'

'Another mistake?' Eva had recovered enough

now to see how grim he looked. And the bleakness in his face wasn't the expression of the replete and happy lover she so wished for him to be!

His mouth thinned. 'I didn't say that—'

'You didn't have to!' Tears of humiliation and hurt burned and blurred Eva's vision as she turned away. 'I think you need to get off me,' she instructed flatly as she kept her face averted from looking directly at Michael, unable to believe that just minutes ago, seconds ago, the two of them had been— That they had been—

Whatever Eva had thought was happening between the two of them she had been wrong. *She* might know herself to be in love with Michael, but his behaviour now, the things he had just said, showed that he had only desired her, and that he now considered even that as having been a mistake.

'I said get off me, Michael!' she repeated forcefully at the same time as she pushed against his chest above her.

'You don't understand—'

'Oh, I understand perfectly, Michael,' she assured him as she stared up at him, using scorn to hide the depth of the hurt she was feeling. 'Now, get off me—'

'I didn't use contraception, Eva!' Michael interrupted harshly as he slowly eased out of her before rolling onto the bed to lie beside her, disgusted with himself for having been so lost in the pleasure of making love with Eva that he hadn't thought to protect her. 'I didn't use contraception...'

This hadn't happened to him since the situation with Emma fourteen years ago, and it shouldn't have happened now either. The last thing— The very last thing that Eva needed in her life right now was an unexpected pregnancy of her own, when she was already exhausted, completely tied, by having to care for her sister's six-month-old twins. It was too soon—would be utterly disastrous if Eva were to have a baby of her own now.

'Eva—'

'Don't!' she warned as she moved sharply away from the hand he had reached out to touch her, her face deathly pale as she sat up on the side of the bed before turning to look back at him scathingly. 'You're in luck, Michael,' she continued scornfully. 'Because, not only am I disease free, but I'm also, for health reasons, currently on the pill.'

Eva could see the relief her assurances had given Michael as he closed his eyes briefly at the same time as he released his breath in a long, satisfied sigh.

She turned away sharply in order to hide the stinging tears that once again blurred her vision. Tears of pain this time. She loved this man, and he— Michael— This was— 'This is even more humiliating than last night.' Eva flatly spoke her thoughts out loud.

'What "health reasons"…?' Michael questioned slowly.

'Nothing serious, just erratic and painful periods,' Eva dismissed unconcernedly. Discussing the intimate workings of her body seemed to be the least of her worries after the intimacies she and Michael had just shared. 'Lucky for you, huh?' she derided dismissively.

'Lucky for both of us,' he corrected softly. 'Eva—'

'I don't intend having a post-mortem about tonight either, Michael!' Eva stood up abruptly before going into the adjoining bathroom, pulling on and fastening her robe over her nakedness before collecting up the rest of her clothes, determined that she wouldn't cry—couldn't allow herself to cry, until she was back in the privacy of her own bedroom.

Thank goodness they hadn't gone to her bedroom in the first place, otherwise she would have the further humiliation of having to sleep in the bed she had briefly shared with Michael, surrounded by the sheets that bore the signs and the intimacy of the scents of their lovemaking.

As it was, no doubt Michael would strip those damp sheets from his own bed, and so eliminate all evidence of this night. Eliminating all evidence that Eva had been in his bed at all…

'Eva—'

'Will you just leave it, Michael?' Eva turned on him fiercely as he tried to talk to her when she re-entered his bedroom, sitting up on the side of the bed now looking across at her with unreadable obsidian eyes. Eva turned away again. 'This was a mistake. My being here at all is a mistake,' she added bleakly. 'And whether you like it or not, I'm booking a flight tomorrow for myself and the twins to return to England.'

He frowned darkly. 'You're right, I don't like it—'

'Tough!' Eva came back unsympathetically. 'Because I assure you that's exactly what's going to happen.'

'You—'

'The subject isn't up for discussion, Michael.' Her eyes flashed briefly in warning before she strode determinedly out of his bedroom and down the hallway to her own room, Michael able to hear the door closing softly behind her just seconds later.

He groaned as he fell back on the bed, knowing he had handled this badly.

That he had handled this whole situation with Eva badly, from start to finish.

And he didn't even try to kid himself that this wasn't the finish for them…

Maybe if he tried to explain about Emma, told Eva what had happened to him in the past, she might understand his distrust of women, this obsession he had for contraception—

No, he answered his own question flatly. If

he had tried to talk to Eva about that now she would only have misunderstood him even further, and the gulf stretching between them would only have widened. If he was going to explain about Emma, and his sordid past, the reason he was always so careful to use contraception—a caution that simply hadn't existed tonight with Eva!—and that his concern tonight had been for her and not him, then he would have to wait until Eva had calmed down.

If she ever did…

CHAPTER ELEVEN

EVA KNEW SHE was just going through the motions the following morning, automatically waking as she responded to hearing the twins calling out to her, before getting up to pull on her robe and going through to the adjoining bedroom, carrying them both through to the kitchen and putting them in their high chairs as she prepared their food, talking to them encouragingly in between bites of their breakfast.

And all the time she did so Eva was totally aware of Michael as he sat broodingly across the kitchen table from her drinking a cup of coffee from the pot he had obviously made earlier, already showered and dressed for work in his dark three-piece business suit and pale blue silk shirt and tie.

As aware as she was that she felt completely numb inside…

Last night had been…beautiful, incredible,

pleasure unlike anything else Eva had ever experienced.

It had also ultimately been more painful than anything she had ever experienced...

Because Michael had made it clear he hadn't made love to her because he was falling in love with her. No, Michael had desired her, and it was a desire he had more than satisfied last night. To the point that his only response afterwards had been to worry about whether or not he might have accidentally made her pregnant by not using contraception!

Well, thank goodness that wasn't even a possibility, because there was no way, after the things Michael had said to her last night, that Eva would ever have told him of that pregnancy even if it had occurred.

As it was, the only thing that interested Eva this morning was booking a flight home for herself and the twins.

'I have no choice but to go into the office for a while this morning.' Michael's voice was huskily low. 'But only long enough to make the arrangements for Pierre to take over my appointments for today, and I would appreciate it if you didn't leave before the two of us have had a chance to speak again.'

Eva raised eyes of dull violet as she looked across the table at him. 'We have nothing left to say to each other.'

'I disagree,' Michael bit out tersely, able to feel the nerve pulsing in his clenched jaw, and knowing, from looking in the mirror as he shaved earlier, that his face was pale and grim this morning.

Not surprising, when he had barely slept all night as he replayed in his mind, over and over again, that last disastrous conversation with Eva.

She shook her head. 'I realised long ago that the only reason you insisted on my staying here with you in the first place was because you wanted to avoid the possibility of my repeating any of my accusations regarding the twins' paternity to anyone else. Don't even try to deny it, Michael, because you and I both know it's the truth,' she warned sharply as he would have spoken.

'Yes,' he sighed in acknowledgement. 'But we've both moved on from there—'

'I haven't,' she assured him flatly. 'And I give you my word that I won't do or say anything more about it until after I hear from either you again or your brother Rafe. But I am leaving today, Michael. Whether you like it or not,' she added firmly, uncompromisingly.

Michael didn't like it, knew there was so much more he and Eva had to say to each other before he could even think of letting her go. Before he could bear to think of her leaving him.

But they were things he needed to say that the determined expression on Eva's face, as she looked across at him so coldly, said that she didn't want to hear from him. Which was a pity, because Michael was just as determined that she would hear him out.

He stood up abruptly. 'I will be back later this morning, Eva, and I would deem it a courtesy to me if you didn't leave until after we've spoken again.'

'A courtesy to you...?' She looked up at him.

'Yes,' he bit out grimly.

That derision now curled the fullness of Eva's lips. Lips that Michael had kissed and enjoyed last night, as he had kissed and enjoyed all of her...!

'Isn't it a little late for formal politeness between the two of us?' she taunted as her thoughts obviously ran along similar lines to his.

Michael's mouth tightened. 'Possibly,' he conceded. 'But I'm asking anyway.'

Eva looked up at him for several more seconds before releasing her breath on a long sigh. 'Okay.' She nodded wearily. 'But that's all I'm agreeing to,' she added sharply. 'I fully intend to book those flights today.'

'The D'Angelo jet—'

'Has absolutely no place in my own or the twins' immediate plans,' Eva assured him sharply, just wishing Michael would go and leave her to suffer her misery in peace; quiet would just be asking too much when in the company of the boisterous twins! 'The sooner you go, Michael, the sooner you'll be back, and then I'll be able to leave,' she added pointedly.

Michael bit back his own sharp reply, knowing now, in the presence of the twins, wasn't the time or the place to have the conversation he and Eva needed to have. 'I should be back in an hour or so.' He nodded tersely.

'Don't rush back on my account,' Eva dismissed.

How, Michael wondered, had the two of them gone from that incredible lovemaking last night to such cold and clipped politeness this morning?

Because he had behaved like an idiot, came the immediate reply. Because he hadn't explained himself to Eva properly last night. Because he should have insisted then that she listen to what he had to say. But hadn't.

And he had no idea whether or not Eva would even allow him to attempt to correct that omission later this morning...

It was almost an hour to the minute later that the doorbell to the apartment rang, Eva placing the twins in the playpen before going to answer it. 'Did you forget your keys—?' She broke off with a frown as she saw that it wasn't Michael standing outside in the hallway.

'Pierre...?' she questioned uncertainly. 'Has something happened to Michael?' she added sharply. She might be angry with him, disappointed in him, but she still loved him, and would be devastated if anything happened to him.

'Mr D'Angelo...?' Pierre repeated with a

puzzled frown. 'No, I—I haven't seen him this morning.'

Eva's eyes widened. 'But he was coming in to the gallery to speak with you...'

Pierre Dupont grimaced. 'I haven't been to the gallery yet this morning either.'

Eva gave a dazed shake of her head. 'Then I don't understand...?'

'No, of course you do not.' The Frenchman sighed heavily as he ran a hand through his already tousled dark hair. 'It is you with whom I wish to speak,' he added grimly.

'Me?' Eva looked at Pierre more closely, realising his appearance was dishevelled. He had a pale face, and a dark growth of unshaven stubble on the squareness of his jaw, and a suit that looked as if he might have slept in it. And his perfect English was no longer as perfect... 'What's this all about, Pierre...?' Eva prompted warily.

'I would rather not discuss it outside in the hallway... May I come in, please?' he prompted huskily. 'I promise I will not take up too much of your time.'

Eva wasn't sure inviting Pierre into Michael's apartment was a good idea, considering the way

Michael had reacted the last time he had caught Eva talking privately with his assistant manager. But as she was still angry with Michael, and leaving Paris later today—she had managed to get three seats on the afternoon flight to England—she didn't particularly care what Michael thought if he should arrive home and find her talking privately with Pierre!

'By all means, come in.' She stepped back to open the door wider, leaving Pierre to enter the apartment and close the door behind him as she hurried back to the sitting room to check on the twins; they had been suspiciously quiet for the past few minutes.

Although what Pierre Dupont could possibly want to discuss with her she had no idea…

Michael was in a foul temper by the time he let himself back into his apartment two hours later, his morning not having gone in the least the way he'd wanted it to. First that stilted conversation with Eva, and her insistence that she was leaving today. Then Pierre hadn't turned up for work, resulting in his having to call Pierre's wife, who had informed him that Pierre wasn't at home, either, so must be on his way to the gallery.

Michael had stayed at the gallery for another half an hour expecting Pierre to arrive with an explanation for his tardiness, aware with every second that ticked by that Eva could even now be on her way to the airport and her flight back to London; he had absolutely no doubt that if there was a flight available Eva would take it, and to hell with his wanting to speak with her before she left!

In the end Michael had just walked out, leaving a slightly perplexed Marie in charge at the gallery while he hurried back to his apartment. And Eva, he hoped.

It was extremely quiet in the apartment as he stepped into the hallway, the sort of empty silence that would once have filled him with satisfaction but today only succeeded in filling him with trepidation. He was too late, Eva had already gone, and the twins with her!

His shoulders dropped in defeat as he entered the sitting room, for a moment not sure he was seeing what he thought he was as he looked at the twins sleeping peacefully in their pushchair, two packed suitcases beside them, and Eva sitting silently in one of the armchairs, as pale and beautiful as a Bellini statue. 'Eva…?' Michael questioned softly.

She turned to look at him, her eyes deep purple wells in the pale alabaster of her face. 'It's all over, Michael.' She spoke flatly, unemotionally.

His heart seemed to somersault in his chest. 'At least give me the chance to explain—'

'There's absolutely nothing for you to explain, Michael,' she assured him in that same unemotional voice. 'Not any more.' She turned away. 'My taxi should be here in a few minutes, but— I'm glad I've had this chance to talk to you before I leave. To apologise.' She drew in a ragged breath. 'You were right, Michael—it wasn't Rafe.'

He looked at her blankly. 'What wasn't Rafe?'

She still didn't look at him as she gave a humourless smile. 'He isn't the twins' father.'

'He isn't?'

'No,' she confirmed tightly.

'How can you possibly know that?'

'Possibly because I had a visit this morning from the man who is!'

Michael gave a dazed shake of his head. 'What?

Who? How would he know to come here?' he questioned sharply. 'No one else even knew you were staying here!'

Eva still couldn't look at Michael but she could hear the confusion in his voice. 'Did you see Pierre at the gallery this morning?' she prompted huskily.

Michael gave a start. 'No, he didn't turn up for work today—Pierre?' he echoed sharply. 'Are you telling me that Pierre is the twins' father?' His eyes were wide with shock.

That was exactly what Eva was telling him!

Pierre Dupont. Married Pierre Dupont. Married and father of two Pierre Dupont. And now—now, it seemed, the father of four!

Eva stood up restlessly. 'Apparently he hadn't realised, had no idea of my connection to Rachel until I mentioned her name yesterday morning. When he looked after the twins for me he noticed—' She breathed deeply. 'He realised then that, apart from the colour of their eyes, Sam and Sophie look very much like his other two children. Which was when he did the maths, and came up with the correct answer that he's the twins' father. He was the one involved with Ra-

chel when she came to Paris last year, Michael,'
she explained as he still looked stunned. 'The
two of them met right here in the gallery, and,
because Pierre is married, he gave her a false
name—'

'Rafe D'Angelo...'

'Yes,' Eva confirmed dully. 'In the certainty,
he said, that there would never be any reason
for her to realise he had lied,' she added bitterly.
'Apparently he's done it before, several times in
fact, and after that first day he always arranges to
meet those women for lunch or dinner well away
from the gallery.' Eva still felt deeply shocked by
Pierre's confession this morning, hadn't so much
as thought of him as a possibility for being the
twins' father. How could she have when Rachel
had told her quite clearly that the father of the
twins was Rafe D'Angelo?

But Eva could visualise it all now, Rachel and
Pierre's initial meeting, the mutual attraction,
the married Pierre giving Rachel a false name so
that he might carry out his illicit affair with the
fun-loving Englishwoman. Now that Eva knew
the truth, the handsome and charming Pierre was

exactly the sort of man Rachel would have been attracted to!

Which explained why, when Eva had thought Michael was Rafe that first day, she'd had such difficulty imagining Rachel and Michael together; Michael was far too complex a character for Rachel's tastes.

But, unfortunately, not Eva's…

She loved Michael with all of those complexities. Maybe because of those complexities; he certainly wasn't a man who would ever bore her, as she had so often been bored by men in the past. As for their lovemaking…! Michael was as complex in that as he was in everything else, which deepened the connection to far beyond the physical. To a degree that Eva knew no other man would ever measure up to the depth of passion and pleasure she had shared with Michael last night.

None of which altered the fact that she had been wrong. That Rafe D'Angelo wasn't the twins' father after all.

That she and the twins had been staying at Michael's apartment under false pretences…

And she couldn't stay here a moment longer,

had to leave, before she broke down completely. 'So I was wrong all along, Michael, and you were right; Rafe isn't the twins' father,' she repeated evenly. 'And I apologise for—for any distress I may have caused you and your family.'

'Eva—'

'The twins and I are booked on the afternoon flight back to England—' she bent to collect her shoulder bag from beside the chair where she had been sitting moments ago '—and the taxi will be arriving any minute to take us to the air-port, so—'

'Eva, I'm sorry!'

She did look at him now, not feeling in the least encouraged by the grimness of Michael's expression as he looked across at her with those unreadable black eyes. 'You have nothing to apol-ogise for, Michael.' She gave a weary shake of her head. 'I made a mistake—God, when I think of the even worse mistake I could have made if you hadn't stopped me!' She groaned achingly. 'I could have just barged into Rafe's life with my accusations and ruined his marriage before it had even begun!'

Michael was very aware of that, had always

been aware of that, which was why he had behaved in the way that he had. But that wasn't
what concerned him now… 'What is Pierre going
to do about this situation?'

Eva closed her eyes, willing the tears not to fall
as she caught her bottom lip briefly between her
teeth. 'I— He has to talk to his wife. Confess all,
I suppose—no hiding the fact that he's a serial
adulterer with the evidence of Sam and Sophie
to prove it!—and see how she reacts to the news
of the twins' existence.'

'How does he think she'll react?'

Eva's smile was bitter as she opened her eyes
again. 'He has absolutely no idea, has apparently
been up all night going over and over in his mind
what he should do. He finally decided to come to
me this morning and confess all.' She grimaced.
'Confessing his infidelities to his wife may be a
little more difficult.'

'Deservedly so,' Michael bit out grimly, disgusted by his assistant manager's behaviour, in
not only using Archangel to meet these other
women, but using his brother's name to do so.

The latter Michael believed the three brothers
should perhaps take some of the blame for; none

of them had ever been at any of the Archangel galleries long enough to have realised Pierre's duplicity. Something Michael intended dealing with when he spoke to his two brothers next, although the fact that they were now all based at a single gallery, Gabriel in London with Bryn, Rafe in New York with Nina, and Michael in Paris, would go a long way to ensure that nothing like this ever happened again.

At the moment it was Eva and the twins who were of prime importance to him. 'What are the options?'

She swallowed again. 'She divorces him, taking his other two children with her. She stays with him, and the two of them continue on as before. Or—or she stays with him and—and agrees to accept the twins into their own family—'

'Over my dead body!' Michael exploded as he crossed the room to lightly grasp the tops of Eva's arms. 'That isn't going to happen, Eva,' he bit out determinedly. 'I simply won't let it.'

She gave a shake of her head. 'Isn't it exactly what you warned me might happen if Rafe was their father?'

'That was before I knew you.' He scowled. 'Before I realised how devoted you are to Sam and Sophie, the sacrifices you've made to keep them.' His expression softened as he looked down at the two sleeping babies. 'You love them as if they were your own.'

'Yes. Well.' Eva cleared her throat as her voice broke emotionally. 'The thing is, they aren't mine.' She sighed. 'And Pierre and his wife have a ready-made family to offer them—'

'A family that consists of a womanising father and a long-suffering wife!'

She gave a stiff shrug of her shoulders. 'And a judge would probably still consider that a better option for the twins' future than a woman on her own.'

'It isn't going to happen, Eva,' Michael bit out grimly.

She looked up at him ruefully. 'I realise you're a powerful man, Michael, but I don't see how even you can stop it if that's what Pierre and his wife decide to do.'

'I'll find a way. No one is taking the twins from you,' Michael assured grimly. 'You love them. They're your children now. They belong with you.'

She smiled sadly. 'It's kind of you to say so after what you initially thought of me—'

'I was wrong, damn it!'

'But it doesn't change the fact that Pierre is their biological father,' Eva continued firmly.

'That has yet to be proven. Maybe—'

'Careful, Michael,' she warned tautly. 'My sister may have been many things—too trusting obviously being one of them, considering the way she fell for Pierre's practised lies—but taking two lovers at the same time was not something she would ever have done. Pierre *is* the twins' father.'

And Michael couldn't accept that Sam and Sophie might be taken away from Eva. Having come to know the three of them, having witnessed Eva's love and devotion to her dead sister's twin babies, and their contentment with her, it was cruel in the extreme to think of them ever being taken away from her.

His mouth tightened. 'How did you leave things with Pierre?'

Eva sighed heavily as she gave a shake of her head. 'I told him that I have every intention of leaving Paris today, and gave him my address in England where he can contact me once he knows what his intentions are.' Tears once again blurred her vision. 'I need to go home to England, Michael. I feel— I feel, probably mistakenly, that there's a sense of safety there for the twins and me.' She was also, Eva knew, hoping that once she was back in her flat in London with the twins she might be able to think of this time spent in Paris as having merely been a bad dream.

A bad dream she had brought completely on herself, Eva accepted, by seeking out the twins' father in the first place...

But she hadn't expected to discover that Rafe D'Angelo wasn't the twins' father, after all.

Any more than she had expected to meet Michael D'Angelo and fall in love with him...

Or to be made to realise quite so painfully, after they had made love last night, that it was a love he would never return.

She blinked back the tears and straightened determinedly as the doorbell to the apartment rang. 'That will be my taxi.'

Michael scowled darkly. 'I'll drive you to the airport—'

'I would rather you didn't,' Eva cut in stiltedly. 'Far better we say our goodbyes here, Michael.' She couldn't quite meet the darkness of his gaze—couldn't look at Michael at all without breaking down completely—so instead gazed sightlessly over his left shoulder. 'You've been very kind—'

'I'm not kind—'

'Yes, you are,' Eva contradicted ruefully. 'Beneath that armour of cold aloofness you're one of the kindest people I've ever known. The twins adore you,' she added, as if that settled the matter. 'I really do have to go now,' she insisted as the doorbell rang for a second time.

Michael felt totally helpless to stop her as he looked at the determination in Eva's expression. 'What about the E J Foster exhibition—?' He broke off with a wince as Eva gave a rueful laugh. 'I can't believe I just said that!'

'You're a businessman first and foremost.' She shrugged as she walked over to take charge of the pushchair. 'If you're still serious about that—'

'I am.'

She nodded. 'Then I'll be in touch.'

'When?' Michael prompted as he carried the two suitcases over to the door for her, knowing his question about the exhibition had nothing to do with business and everything to do with his seeing Eva again.

'I really don't know.' She sighed. 'Everything is so up in the air at the moment—I'll call you,' she said again as she opened the door to greet the taxi driver.

'I'll bring the cases down—'

'I really would rather you didn't, Michael.' Eva turned to look at him, tears shimmering in those violet-coloured eyes as she reached up on tip-toe and kissed him lightly on the cheek. 'I hate protracted goodbyes, don't you?' she murmured before she followed the taxi driver down the hall-way to the lift without so much as a glance back at Michael.

Michael had never really thought about it be-fore now, but he did know, as Eva and the twins got into the lift, that he hated *this* goodbye, at least. That he didn't want to say goodbye to Eva at all!

Or the twins…

He had grown fond of the little rascals over the past few days of helping care for them, knew his apartment was going to have the oppressive si-lence of a morgue once they, and Eva, had gone.

Most especially Eva...

With this need for a hurried departure to the airport, Michael hadn't so much as had chance to talk to Eva about the misunderstandings of last night, and he certainly couldn't talk about it now she had left!

Besides which, Michael fully intended to sort out this situation with Pierre before talking to Eva again...

CHAPTER TWELVE

'MICHAEL...?' EVA'S EYES opened wide as she didn't even attempt to hide her surprise, after opening the door to her flat to find him standing outside in the hallway of the slightly shabby Victorian building she had lived in for the past three years.

It had been four days since she had left Paris—and Michael—and flown back to England with the twins. Four very long and oppressive days, when she had missed Michael as much, if not more, than she had dreaded hearing from Pierre Dupont again, in regard to the twins' future.

So far there had been complete silence from Pierre, lulling Eva into—what she was sure was a false hope!—thinking that maybe he had decided not to do anything about them, that things could just continue the way they had been, and the twins would stay with her. Ridiculous, perhaps, but even so it was all that had kept Eva from going quietly insane.

Seeing Michael again—literally visually eating up his casual appearance in a pale blue shirt unfastened at the throat and worn beneath a black soft suede jacket, and faded denims—was more wonderful than she could ever have imagined. And she had imagined seeing Michael again a lot!

Had missed being with him beyond that imagining.

Loved him beyond imagining too...

'Are you going to invite me inside...?' he prompted gruffly.

'Of course.' Eva stepped back in order to open the door wider so that he could step into the hallway before she closed the door behind him, instantly aware of how tall and wide-shouldered—and immediate—he appeared in the narrow confines of the hallway. 'Come through to the sitting room,' she invited as she stepped past him to lead the way.

'Have I arrived at nap time...?' Michael prompted ruefully as he looked around the deserted and silent sitting room. A room that so obviously reflected the warmth of Eva's personality, the colours an amalgam of warm russets to cream, with multicoloured cushions on the sofa and chairs, several of her own framed photographs adorning the walls.

'How did you guess?' She chuckled softly as she indicated he should sit down in one of those armchairs.

Michael remained standing as he turned from looking at those photographs in order to study Eva more closely, noting the deepened shadows beneath her eyes, and the fact that her face seemed thinner than ever, no doubt a sign that worry over the twins' future had caused her to lose weight since he had last seen her. Unless… 'Are the twins both well?' he prompted concernedly.

'Very much so.' Eva lightly dispelled that worry.

'Good.' He nodded his satisfaction. 'And you?'

She grimaced. 'I'm as well as can be expected when I still haven't heard anything from Pierre.'

Michael straightened. 'That's one of the reasons I'm here.'

She tensed warily. 'It is?'

He nodded grimly. 'Pierre has decided to give up any and all rights to the twins and allow you to formally adopt them, if that's agreeable to you?'

Relief washed over Eva, hot tears welling in her eyes and spilling unchecked down her cheeks, her knees feeling suddenly weak and causing her to stagger blindly over to drop down heavily into one of the armchairs before she buried her face in her hands and began to sob in earnest.

'Eva...?'

'I'm okay.' She waved away Michael's concern even as she tried to mop up the worst of the tears. 'I just— You didn't coerce him or force him in any way, did you?' she prompted suspiciously as she realised that maybe this solution to the problem that had kept her awake for so many nights was perhaps just too good to be true.

Michael gave a humourless smile. 'I would have done everything in my power to do exactly that if Pierre hadn't come to me yesterday and told me that he and his wife have spoken at length on the subject, for the last three days apparently, and that the two of them have decided to give their obviously rocky marriage another go. But not with the twins as a constant reminder of Pierre's infidelity. Something I could have—should have—telephoned and told you yesterday,' he added, 'rather than wait until today so that I could come here and tell you in person.'

Eva was just too relieved at the news to care when she was told. 'He won't change his mind...?' she prompted uncertainly.

'He assures me that he won't,' Michael said hardly. 'And, as I no longer require his services at any of the Archangel galleries, I've arranged a...change of employment for him, as another incentive for him to keep to that decision.'

'What sort of change of employment?' Eva prompted uncertainly.

Michael shrugged. 'Believe it or not the world of art galleries and auction houses is a relatively small one, and Pierre is intelligent enough to know that if I chose to do so then I could ensure that he never works in another gallery again. Anywhere,' he added grimly.

'And that isn't coercion?'

'Not in the least, when I didn't make the arrangements until after he had told me his decision regarding Sam and Sophie,' Michael dismissed.

'Which was when I told him that my own decision is that he will never work in an Archangel gallery ever again.' He grimaced with distaste. 'He saw the…practicality of my suggestion, once I'd told him that I would arrange for him to work in another gallery elsewhere. Apparently he's always wanted to work and live in Rome, and feels that it would be better for his marriage if he and his wife were to start somewhere completely afresh. Whether that's true or not remains to be seen, but in the meantime I have no intention of allowing him the time to change his mind where the twins are concerned.'

'How do you intend stopping him?' Eva looked up at him slightly dazed, thrilled at the idea of the twins being completely hers, and so grateful to Michael for what he had done for her. For them, she reminded herself, because Michael had done this for the twins as much as for her.

'Immediately after Pierre told me of his decision I contacted the lawyers who act for our galleries in Paris and London, instructing them to liaise on the application for the formal adoption of the twins,' Michael revealed huskily. 'Those papers are now waiting at the lawyers' office in London to be signed and formally submitted.'

Eva could barely breathe, had no idea what to think, knowing that, despite all her false accusations of paternity the previous week, Michael had still done this for her and the twins.

Tears once again blurred her vision, but they were happy tears this time. The twins were going to be truly hers, so that no one, and nothing, could ever take them away from her again.

'And you said you aren't kind!' she reminded teasingly through the falling of those happy tears.

'I'm truly not,' he denied ruefully.

'You truly are!'

He looked at her intently. 'And if I were to tell you that my reasons for doing any and all of those things, even being here today, are completely selfish ones...?'

Eva gave a puzzled shake of her head. 'What could you possibly hope to gain by helping me to adopt the twins?'

The moment of truth, Michael realised. The reason he was here today. The reason he hadn't been able to stay away a moment longer...

His Parisian apartment had been every bit as

much like a morgue as Michael had expected it would be after Eva's departure: silent, cold, and empty. So empty.

He had filled his days with work at the gallery, of course, but each evening he had returned to his apartment, knowing that Eva wouldn't be there, that the twins wouldn't be there. And he had hated it. Every damned moment of it.

He had felt as if he were truly damned and bereft without Eva's sunny personality and warmth to come home to, without the twins' antics to laugh about with her.

And he couldn't stand the distance yawning between them another moment longer, so moved down on his haunches beside Eva's chair before taking one of her hands in his. 'Eva—' He broke off, his voice very hoarse as his fingers lightly caressed hers. 'There's one detail on the adoption application that hasn't been filled in yet.'

'Oh?' Her expression became wary again.

'Nothing for you to worry about,' he assured firmly. 'I just—I wanted—Eva, you misunderstood me the other evening!'

And warier still… 'About what?' she prompted distantly.

Michael released her hand to stand up restlessly. 'I didn't—I wasn't—' Damn it, this indecisiveness wasn't like him! 'The reason for my concern, about our not having used contraception that night, was for your benefit, not mine,' he bit out forcefully. 'You already have the twins, and they're so young still, and I thought an unexpected pregnancy of your own would be a very bad idea right now.'

Her cheeks were flushed a fiery red, her gaze no longer meeting his. 'You're right, a very bad idea. For you as well as me. Which is why—why I quickly assured you that you had no need to worry about it—'

'I told you, I'm not worried on my own account, Eva,' he insisted fiercely. 'We could have another set of twins immediately for all I care. Three sets! We would cope. I just—' He thrust his hands into the pockets of his denims. 'I didn't—I don't want it to happen like that for you. For us,' he added huskily.

Questioningly, it seemed to Eva, almost afraid to hope, and yet knowing that hope was growing, building inside her, nonetheless.

She swallowed before speaking. 'I don't understand...'

Michael drew in a harsh breath. 'There's something I need to tell you, and ask you in a moment, but first I want to explain about something that happened to me fourteen years ago—'

'You don't owe me any explanations—'

'I was twenty-one at the time,' he continued determinedly. 'One of the three eligible D'Angelo brothers, slightly wild, slightly naïve, and no doubt more than slightly full of myself— Oh, yes, Eva,' he drawled as she gave a disbelieving snort, 'I think I was probably all of those things then.' He grimaced. 'Anyway, I became involved with someone while at university. Her name was Emma. We had a good time together, and I thought I was in love. And when she came to me one day and told me that she was pregnant, I— No, this isn't a pretty story, Eva,' he acknowledged grimly as she gasped.

Not pretty, no, but Eva was starting to suspect it might be the reason for Michael's distrust of women, and surely responsible for his instant and assured denial of her initial claim as to his being the twins' father, when she had mistakenly thought he was Rafe D'Angelo. It had already happened to Michael once, and it wasn't something he would ever risk happening again.

Except he had…

With her.

Oh, she might not be pregnant, her pill having ensured that she wasn't, but Michael hadn't known that at the time…

'Go on,' she encouraged softly.

He nodded. 'I asked her to marry me. We were making plans for the wedding when she met someone else, someone wealthier, older, and decided that he was a much better prospect as a husband. The—the baby miraculously disappeared overnight.'

'God…!' Eva breathed softly.

'I told you it wasn't a particularly pretty story.' Michael sighed at his naiveté all those years ago. 'It's the oldest trick in the book, I'm told.'

'She was lying the whole time…'

'Yes,' he acknowledged grimly. 'She tried the same trick on the new man she'd met, and was furious when I warned him what she was up to. None of which is important now—' he straightened dismissively '—except I hope it might explain some of my behaviour this past week?' He looked at her searchingly. 'I was distrustful when you arrived with the twins, first claiming they were mine and then that they were Rafe's, and I made accusations that I'm sincerely ashamed of—'

'I understand the reason for that now.' Eva understood so much of Michael's previous behaviour now; was it any wonder he had been so suspicious of her motives after this girl Emma had tried to trick him into marriage with a false pregnancy all those years ago?

'Yes. But I want you to know that has nothing to do with my worry over our not having used contraception the night we made love together,' he continued decisively. 'As I told you just now, we can have half a dozen sets of twins as far as I'm concerned. I just don't want that for you right now.'

'You said you had something else to tell me and something to ask me…?' she reminded huskily, still too afraid to truly hope.

'Yes.'

'And?' she prompted tensely when he remained silent.

'And I've fallen in love with you!' The words burst out of him, as if from lack of use. 'I love you, Eva.' It seemed easier for him to say the second time, the darkness of his eyes glowing with the emotion. 'The last four days without you have been—they've been hell on earth!' He gave a shake of his head, his expression bleak. 'I can't think, can't sleep for thinking of you, wanting to be with you. As for the apartment—! I couldn't stand spending another single day or night there when everywhere I look, every room I go into, reminds me of you, and your being there with the twins. With me.'

The hope Eva had been holding in check now blossomed, burst free, and she rose quickly to her feet to go to Michael, hating that look of desolation on his dear beloved face. 'I love you too, Michael.' She raised a tentative hand to his cheek. 'I love you so much, and it hurts so much not being with you!'

'Eva…!' His eyes glowed down into hers like black onyx as he swept her up into his arms and kissed her.

Eva had no idea how much later it was when they finally surfaced long enough to be able to talk again, having been too lost in the wonder of loving Michael and knowing that he loved her in return to notice the passing of time.

'Will you marry me, Eva?'

She looked up at Michael uncertainly as they lay together on the sofa. 'The twins—'

'Will be ours,' Michael assured firmly.

Eva gave a pained frown. 'Are you sure? It's an awfully big responsibility to take on someone else's children—'

'As you should know, but they'll be our children, Eva. That's if you'll agree to marry me…?' he prompted uncertainly. 'I don't want some brief relationship with you, Eva, I want to know that you'll be mine. For always.'

'I am yours, for always.' Eva had no doubt that the love she had for Michael, that he had for her, was a tried and tested love, the sort of love that would last and endure.

'Then marry me,' he urged huskily. 'Eva, the only detail missing from the adoption papers is the names of the adoptive parents, and I would deem it a great privilege if you would allow my name to appear next to yours…'

'Oh, Michael!' Eva choked back the tears. 'Yes,'

she cried. 'Yes, yes, yes.' She covered his face with happy kisses.

'Is that a yes to marrying me or a yes to my adopting the twins with you?'

'Both!' She beamed up at him.

'I was hoping you would say that!' Michael's arms tightened about her possessively. 'I promise to love you for the rest of our lifetime, Eva Foster,' he vowed fiercely.

'And I promise to love you for the same lifetime, Michael D'Angelo—' She broke off as one of the twins let out a cry. 'Oops.' Eva chuckled ruefully as she sat up. 'This could be the story of our life, you know, baby *interruptus*!'

'I'm looking forward to every moment of it!' he assured as he stood up with her to go to Sam and Sophie.

So was Eva.

So was Eva…

EPILOGUE

Four weeks later, St Mary's Church, London.

'IT REALLY IS a case of how the mighty have fallen this time, isn't it?' Rafe remarked lightly to Gabriel as the two men sat beside each other on the front pew of the church.

'More like the felling of a giant oak tree that's been standing strong and unmoving for hundreds of years,' Gabriel came back dryly. 'Who would ever have thought that Michael would not only fall in love but also become the father of twins in just a few short weeks? And now he's getting married too!'

'And after mocking our own recent demise.' Rafe nodded.

'I'm not taking any notice of either of you,' Michael drawled unconcernedly as he sat closest to the aisle waiting for Eva to appear in the church, his two brothers beside him acting as his best men. 'As long as I have Eva as my wife and the twins as our children I'm going to remain totally immune to your teasing in future!' The three brothers were all settled into their respective galleries now, Gabriel in London, Rafe in New York, Michael in Paris, all of them determined that nothing like the Pierre episode should ever happen again in their name.

'We aren't teasing, Michael, not really. We're just happy for you,' Gabriel assured sincerely.

'We truly are,' Rafe echoed just as sincerely. 'Eva is beautiful. And the two of you are perfect for each other.'

'Thank you,' Michael accepted softly.

'And we aren't just saying that because you managed to secure the second E J Foster exhibition as well as a wife!' Rafe couldn't resist adding teasingly.

'Enjoy it while you can, Rafe, but I'm going to have the last laugh...' Michael assured dryly.

'How so?' Gabriel prompted cautiously.

Michael grinned unabashedly. 'It was my suggestion that Eva have Bryn and Nina as her bridesmaids, and it was a stroke of genius on her part to have Bryn carry Sophie as the third bridesmaid, and Nina carry Sam as the ring-bearer. The two of them fell instantly in love with the little darlings, and I have no doubt that the two of you are going to be in for some serious wheedling about having children of your own later this evening!'

'Fine with me,' Rafe murmured smugly.

'Me too.' Gabriel nodded happily.

'God, we're a sappy lot, aren't we?' Michael murmured ruefully. He thought about the house they were in the process of buying in Paris, with a garden for the twins to play in.

'And happy to be so—' Rafe broke off what he had been about to say as the organist began to play the wedding march, the three brothers rising quickly to their feet.

Michael turned proudly to watch as his bride, as his beloved Eva, walked down the aisle towards him, a vision in white satin and lace, their love shining brightly as they gazed into each other's eyes.

The love of a lifetime.

And a lifetime to love…

* * * * *

Mills & Boon® Large Print

August 2014

A D'ANGELO LIKE NO OTHER
Carole Mortimer

SEDUCED BY THE SULTAN
Sharon Kendrick

WHEN CHRISTAKOS MEETS HIS MATCH
Abby Green

THE PUREST OF DIAMONDS?
Susan Stephens

SECRETS OF A BOLLYWOOD MARRIAGE
Susanna Carr

WHAT THE GREEK'S MONEY CAN'T BUY
Maya Blake

THE LAST PRINCE OF DAHAAR
Tara Pammi

THE SECRET INGREDIENT
Nina Harrington

STOLEN KISS FROM A PRINCE
Teresa Carpenter

BEHIND THE FILM STAR'S SMILE
Kate Hardy

THE RETURN OF MRS JONES
Jessica Gilmore

Mills & Boon® Large Print

September 2014

THE ONLY WOMAN TO DEFY HIM
Carol Marinelli

SECRETS OF A RUTHLESS TYCOON
Cathy Williams

GAMBLING WITH THE CROWN
Lynn Raye Harris

THE FORBIDDEN TOUCH OF SANGUARDO
Julia James

ONE NIGHT TO RISK IT ALL
Maisey Yates

A CLASH WITH CANNAVARO
Elizabeth Power

THE TRUTH ABOUT DE CAMPO
Jennifer Hayward

EXPECTING THE PRINCE'S BABY
Rebecca Winters

THE MILLIONAIRE'S HOMECOMING
Cara Colter

THE HEIR OF THE CASTLE
Scarlet Wilson

TWELVE HOURS OF TEMPTATION
Shoma Narayanan

0814 Rom LP

RJ